ILLIBERAL EDUCATION

A NOVEL

LLOYD J. AVERILL

PAN PRESS

2

For Carol
who first had the idea

ACKNOWLEDGMENTS

It is with pleasure and gratitude that I acknowledge the critical assistance of a number of people during the writing of this novel. Chief among them is a group of friends from the University Congregational United Church of Christ, Seattle, who, on three afternoons at the Seabeck Conference Center on Hood Canal in 1996, heard excerpts from an early draft and gave me the benefit of their immediate assessments. Individuals who have read the manuscript and generously shared with me their critical comments include Laurence Barrett, Eric Dean Bennett, Lara Bennett, Jennifer Brandon, Catherine Fransson, Peter Ilgenfritz, Judith Kelson, Lorinda Koller, Rebecca Magnus, Elizabeth Mitchell, Daphne Morris, Katie Pasco, David Shull, and Peggy Williams. They have my warm thanks, as does Paul McArdle, who gave me valued assistance with the design of the book. Jessie Kenton of Pan Press facilitated the publication with her usual good humor and helpfulness.

Carol White urged me, some years ago, to "Try your hand at writing fiction. You might be good at it." Whatever readers may think of the prescience of her prediction, I am indebted to her for the suggestion, since it has provided me with the most fun I have ever had in a 40-year career in writing. It is to her that the book is dedicated.

Passages in Chapter 1 by Albert Camus are from *The Rebel, An Essay on Man in Revolt*, translated by Anthony Bower (Vintage Books, 1956), pp. 249-250.

Reference in Chapter 3 to biblical scholarship that sees Jesus substituting a new "politics of compassion" for the older "politics of purity" is primarily to the work of Marcus Borg, *Jesus, A New Vision: Spirit, Culture, and the Life of Discipleship* (HarperSanFrancisco, 1987), and *Meeting Jesus Again for the First Time: The Historical Jesus and the Heart of Contemporary Faith*, (HarperSanFrancisco, 1994), especially Chapter 3.

A quotation from Reinhold Niebuhr in Chapter 5 is from *Moral Man and Immoral Society: A Study in Ethics and Politics* (Charles Scribner's Sons, 1932), p. xi f.

The prayer by Frederick Buechner in Chapter 15 is from *The Hungering Dark* (Seabury Press, 1981), pp. 88-89.

FOREWORD

Over the years I have been a teacher and administrator in five colleges, in some respects not unlike the one that is the setting for *Illiberal Education, A Novel*—small, undergraduate, church-related, liberal arts—in places that include Florida, West Virginia, Michigan, Illinois, and Kansas. Inevitably, then, my experiences in those places have shaped the profile of my fictional Macauley College, and have informed the issues with which characters in the novel struggle. But no actual persons or places are depicted.

Fortunately for me, and for the students and teachers in those five colleges, none was bedeviled—I use the term advisedly—either by homophobia or by opportunistic religious conservatism. They had problems enough of their own, without these two.

And after some 30 years in intimate association with such places, I still believe that, however flawed the actual practice of the private, undergraduate, liberal arts college may be, it is potentially the most effective environment for the humanistic teaching and learning of younger adults. It is, indeed, America's most distinctive, most admirable contribution to the world of higher education.

This novel is about a college that was on the verge of failing its liberating promise. The fact that we know it was in danger of failing suggests that the image of what it ought to have been, could have been, still lives.

But while the collegiate setting for the novel is of its essence, it is not in the end primarily a novel about the vagaries of academic life. Not until I had finished writing it did I discover what this novel is really about, and then only when a friend demanded of me a kind of "twenty-five-words-or-less" summary of it. Then I realized that it is, in fact, an account of the search for human authenticity and integrity—in short, for personal wholeness—by two of its characters; of the painful process from which one of the characters had already emerged in her own search; and of the unwelcome opportunity for self-knowledge that circumstances foisted, willy-nilly, upon three others.

In this way, rather than being a novel about academic life, it is instead an extended metaphor for the larger life-process in which we are all engaged. Each of us has known those three modes of experience, sometimes *seriatim*, sometimes in painful combination, and in their midst we have known the sharpness of our disappointments and the exhilaration of our satisfactions.

It may even be possible that the story that follows will find a place in the reader's own quest for wholeness. That would be the most rewarding outcome an author could possibly derive from his writing.

Lloyd J. Averill
Seattle, Washington

ABOUT THE AUTHOR

Among Lloyd J. Averill's twelve other books are works on higher education, sociology, theology, and Northwest Coast Native art history.

Since 1951 he has taught religious studies at both undergraduate and graduate levels, and is now senior lecturer emeritus in the University of Washington.

This is his first novel.

FRIDAY

CHAPTER ONE
OFF *to a* BAD START

It was ten minutes to eight when Lane Thomas left the house. He knew he would be late, and he wasn't sure the students would still be in the classroom when he arrived. They had this crazy notion that they were only required to wait ten minutes for an Assistant Professor, somewhat longer for teachers of more elevated professorial standing.

There was certainly nothing about it in the Academic Handbook. It was pure student mythology, passed on annually from sophomores to freshmen. Of course, it was even more effective that way. It would have been ignored if it had been in the Academic Handbook, which nobody—students or faculty—ever read.

Besides, the students in that eight-o'clock class were a sullen lot. Perhaps it had something to do with the early hour. He remembered the old saying about how students chose their courses: nothing before 10 o'clock, nothing above the first floor. Even though his course on "Theological Issues in Contemporary Literature" was an elective and consequently the students were there by choice, they seemed to take special pleasure in a passive resistance to his effort to find common existential questions in uncommon pairs of thinkers and their works: French literary man Jean-Paul Sartre paired with German-American theologian Paul Tillich; Graham Greene's *The Heart of the Matter* with Dietrich Bonhoeffer's *Letters and Papers from Prison*; Albert Camus' *The Fall* with H. Richard Niebuhr's *The Meaning of Revelation*.

He was merely trying to offer them a serious intellectual game, to unearth in them some buried shard of curiosity, but for the most part this was a singularly incurious bunch.

So they would be acting true to form if they were to vacate the classroom on the dot of 8:10, scattering to the Campus Union or back to the dorm beds from which they had so recently and reluctantly emerged for this earliest class of the day.

He didn't need this. Word would get around quickly that the class had walked out on him, and it would scarcely help his chances for achieving tenure before this academic year was up. It was well known that teacher reputations played an informal but influential role in tenure decisions.

More than that, formal student evaluations of teaching were standard items to be included in a tenure dossier, and his late arrival would only add to their sullen assessment of him, particularly since he had promised the return today of graded term papers for which they thought they had already waited much too long.

He had overslept because he was at the computer until 3:30 a.m., putting the finishing touches on a meticulously detailed *curriculum vitae*, the last item to be prepared but the frontispiece to that damned dossier, which was due in his department chairman's office that very afternoon.

Despite the lateness of the hour, with only four hours of sleep he found it difficult to rouse his 5'10" frame into action, much less to move it quickly, and he stumbled about the bedroom looking for some reasonably coherent combination of pants, shirt, and jacket for his classroom appearance, struggling into a top coat as he went out the front door.

Tenure, Lane thought as he hurried toward the classroom building: that was his real *bete noir*, the dark pall that had hung over his life for long weeks like a smothering fog. Putting the required dossier together had become an all-consuming work, compromising time for lecture preparation at the very moment when he needed to be at his classroom best; making for preoccupied days and sleepless nights; alienating friends for whom he had had almost no time since spring.

The students were right about those term papers, of course. For maximum educational usefulness, he should have returned them with his thoughtful annotations a week after they had been handed in. But those papers had taken second place to gathering copies of his own published articles from the last six years, listing the conferences at which he had made scholarly presentations, seeking letters of commendation from professional colleagues in other colleges, and demonstrating his indispensability to this college by active and responsible membership on faculty committees and participation in the wider community beyond the campus.

And what would all that get him? Macauley College was trying to ride the wave of conservatism, currently abroad in the country, to a new academic prosperity in students and fundraising. Established by Baptists in the mid-nineteenth century wave of Christian-college founding, through most of its more recent history the college had cordially ignored those religious origins at worst, or nominally acknowledged them at a reluctant best.

But three years ago a new president, Charles Kean, son of an ultra-conservative Baptist minister, whose first act was to enlist as Trustees a substantial group of wealthy churchmen of like mind, had decided with them that the college's future lay in becoming aggressively and conservatively religious.

Early in the new regime, several developments signaled a move to the religious and political right. One was the creation, with the first major endowment gift, of a Center for Christian Freedom, designed to assist churches in this Midwest region in mobilizing their resources in support of Christian school board candidates, campaigns for prayer in the schools, opposition to local abortion activities, and the like. Macauley students were to be trained to be trainers in the outreach activities of the Center.

Another was an announcement that, over a four-year period, resort to federal scholarship funds would be phased out, and a "Campaign for Independence" was inaugurated in the hope of riding the current anti-federal government mood and of attracting increased financial support from right-wing individuals and foundations.

Within the College, there was increasing pressure on the faculty from President and Trustees to establish a "Christian Values" core of academic studies, including certain required courses in religion, sociology, and economics—though this had not yet happened.

Lane had arrived before that sea change occurred, and he often reflected that, had he applied a year or two later, probably he would not have been appointed. Although in theological outlook an Episcopalian of evangelical persuasion, he was one of the "new" evangelicals. While holding to the main tenets of Christian orthodoxy, this newer breed was eager to dissociate itself from the extremes of fundamentalist biblicism, dogmatism, and separatism from the mainstream of intellectual culture. Positively, they sought to play a mediating role between the extremes of the theological right and the old-line denominations, and to take up the social justice issues that seemed the simple outcomes of the teaching of Jesus.

After completing a combined undergraduate major in literature and religion at Oregon's Presbyterian-related Lewis and Clark College, Lane took his doctorate at Claremont, with its reputation for Process Theology, generally regarded as the left-wing of the theological enterprise. Given the current predilections of Macauley's decision makers, the fact that he had not attended what they viewed as "safe" institutions meant that, even as an evangelical, he was considered as unreliable, at best, in a college that now preferred a more overtly right-wing confessional stance. And to top it all off, he was an Episcopalian! Conservative Baptists had never felt very comfortable with prayer books, vestments, and bishops.

The new Religion Department chairman, hand-picked three years ago by Macauley's president and appointed at the rank of full professor with tenure, wanted teachers like himself, who could be paraded before the Trustees as exemplars of the college's fashionable and aggressive new religiosity.

Given this current situation, what chance had he for tenure, he worried, however exemplary by other criteria his dossier might be?

He ran through the campus Quad, turned into Founders Hall, and took the steps two at a time to his second-floor office to grab up the promised term papers on his way to the nearby classroom. His office door bore a white card with the legend:

Lane Thomas, Ph.D.

Assistant Professor of Religion

Office hours: M-W-F, 10:30-Noon

Home tel.: 778-3686

Including a home telephone wasn't common practice among his faculty colleagues. Some even had their numbers unlisted by the telephone company in order to discourage out-of-class contacts with students. Somehow that had always seemed to him the mark of a time-server, not of an educator.

Much as he valued his privacy, real learning, real excitement about ideas, had come to him as a contagion from his own teachers at Lewis and Clark College, accessible men and women who thought education couldn't be quarantined to the classroom, and who had given him more of themselves than mere lectures could contain. Difficult as it had been to sustain against a prevailing faculty culture at Macauley that preferred its own convenience, he had intended from his first day of teaching to be that kind of educator, and the telephone number on the card was a small earnest of his intent.

Term papers in hand but the time now past the mythological ten-minute limit, he headed for the classroom. It would probably be empty, he thought.

Except perhaps for one—Lise Warner, daughter of an unpleasantly conservative clergyman recently appointed chairman of the Board of Trustees. Lise always sat in the first row, directly in front of the podium. When he lectured, she never seemed to take her eyes from his face. Did she never take notes? Yet her answers on examinations were unexceptionable. Lise troubled him, stirred something in him that was as yet unformed.

He opened the classroom door and stepped apprehensively in. She was there.

CHAPTER TWO

A DISTURBING PRESENCE

It had all begun innocently enough. Perhaps it was still all innocence. Why wasn't he sure about that?

Although Lane had searched his feelings repeatedly, he still couldn't find the source of the strange inner movement he experienced whenever he became aware of Lise Warner's steady brown eyes, her undivided attention; still couldn't decide what his real feelings were about her, and what was merely self-deception.

Not that there was anything unusual in his male, 32-year-old appreciation of a very attractive, 21-year-old female. She was of medium height for a woman, perhaps 5' 6", and "lithe" was the word that came to Lane when he thought about her physical presence. Shoulder-length dark hair was touched with natural auburn highlights, and those brown eyes had a depth that seemed to draw him in.

There was surely nothing wrong in admitting, at least to himself, how attractive he found her to be. He was single and had no special attachments, except for occasional dates with Anne Armstrong, a faculty friend in Political Science. Determined to complete his doctoral dissertation by the second year of his teaching at Macauley, and then devoting his full energies to developing a reputation as a promising teacher and scholar in anticipation of tenure, he simply hadn't been willing to take the time that serious romantic entanglements demand.

At least, that was what he had told himself. But true as it was, Lane knew that it wasn't the whole truth. His relationships with women had always been problematic, beginning with a widowed mother who had expected him to meet her emotional needs with little thought for what his own adolescent needs might be. During undergraduate years at Lewis and Clark, he had fallen under the three-year spell of a beautiful and strong-willed classmate. Emotional commitments had always been difficult for him, and by the time he had been able to screw up his courage to entertain the possibility of a longer-term relationship with her, she had lost interest in him and had moved on to someone else. After his months-long build-up to commitment, the break was devastating to Lane, and he plunged at once into a demanding and distracting program of graduate study. During its five years he had not dated at all, and in fact he had only begun to reach out tentatively to Anne Armstrong a year ago.

Now with his work on tenure done, it was only natural that he should think of devoting to his personal life some of the energy and attention his professional life had been claiming.

But Lise Warner was a special case. There was something more than ordinarily disturbing about his response to her, and a vague awareness that, if he were not careful, he might find himself edging toward an inviolable faculty-student boundary.

He had not noticed her at all when the semester began. In fact, he was quite unaware of her attentiveness until she called him one evening, using the home telephone number he had posted on his office door. She asked for an appointment to discuss some ideas in assigned reading that she had found both fascinating and troubling.

The reading was from Albert Camus' *The Rebel*, and its view of meaning and meaninglessness had challenged the received wisdom she had brought with her to college. So of course he had agreed to meet her, suggesting conversation over coffee in the Campus Union on the following afternoon.

After conventional openers to ease their mutual awkwardness—predictions about the prospects for Macauley's nationally-ranked soccer team, a brief comment on a recently promulgated residence hall regulation that was agitating the editors of the student newspaper—she introduced the presenting issue for their meeting.

"Dr. Thomas," she began, "I find Camus' apparent rejection of history upsetting and, in a strange way, promising at the same time. I've always been taught to respect history—especially my own Western, Christian, family history; to accept it as the only source of values and standards worth trusting and therefore not to question its authority over my life. But see here. I'm not sure I understand what Camus is saying—and if I understand it, what I ought to think about it."

She pointed to a paragraph in the chapter on "Historical Rebellion":

> ...history alone offers no hope. It is not a source of values but is still a source of nihilism....Thought that is derived from history alone, like thought that rejects history completely, deprives man of the means and the reason for living. The former drives him to the extreme decadence of "why live?" the latter to "how live?" History, necessary but not sufficient, is therefore only an occasional cause. It is not absence of values, nor values themselves, nor even the source of values. It is one occasion, among others, for man to prove the still confused existence of a value that allows him to judge history. Rebellion itself makes us the promise of such a value.

"There's more, too," she added before Lane Thomas could respond. "Look, here in the next paragraph."

> ...rebellion, in man, is the refusal to be treated as an object and to be reduced to simple historical terms. It is the affirmation of a nature common to all men, which eludes the world of power. History, undoubtedly, is one of the limits of man's experience; in this sense the revolutionaries are right. But man, by rebelling, imposes in his turn a limit on history, and at that limit the promise of a value is born.

"Dr. Thomas," Lise pressed, "does that mean that each of us...that I must become a rebel against my own history?"

Lane Thomas was torn. Her earnestness and eagerness touched him. It was clear that her questions weren't mere excuses for impressing a student's intellectual seriousness upon her teacher. There was too much concern, even passion, in her tone. He sensed that something more was there, and he was uncertain whether to address the presenting issue or to probe for the more that might be underneath.

He decided to take a cautious approach, hoping to reach the hidden root of her concern, if there were one, by taking her spoken (and implied) questions seriously.

"I can understand how these statements of Camus' might be troubling," Lane Thomas said. "Most of us in this college, teachers as well as students, were shaped early by the same views you report. We were taught that all important precedents have already been set, that we ought to yield to the superior authority of tradition, and that rebellion is synonymous with destructiveness.

"Of course," he went on, "colleges are not commonly viewed that way. We are identified in the public mind with nay-sayers and rebels. I once heard a college president define a professor as 'a man who thinks otherwise.' And it's true that a college campus gives us a bit of room to do that, more room than in other parts of society, so faculties have their share of nay-sayers. And student newspapers have their share of editors who mimic that fashionable faculty style.

"But the truth is that we are all pretty timid, pretty tentative rebels, given more to verbal daring than to anything else, and in the end unwilling to change anything that would really disturb the essential order of things.

"And that's too bad," said Lane. "Because, as Camus saw so clearly, when we fail in radical criticism of history, including our own history, we permit it to tyrannize over our individual selfhood and to set us in a willing concentration camp.

"One of the differences between Camus and us is that he really dared to be a rebel and didn't hesitate to live fully in its disturbing consequences."

Lane paused. "There is a somewhat less extreme view of history, one perhaps more accessible to you, in another of our assigned readings. In *The Meaning of Revelation*, H. Richard Niebuhr talks about the relativity of all of our historical apprehensions. Truth, including historical truth, the truth of our received history, isn't always and everywhere the same. Rather it is always and everywhere relative—relative to time and to place. But that needn't be a source of despair for us; that needn't lead us to the conclusion that nothing is permanent. Even if we never have absolute truth, said Niebuhr, we may nevertheless have truth about the absolute."

Lane Thomas paused again. "By the way," he said, "how are things at home?"

This sudden change of direction obviously took Lise quite by surprise, and for a moment her eyes had a startled look. Then Lane saw tears beginning to form, and he looked away to ease any self-consciousness she might feel at this overt evidence of some new emotion.

His question wasn't premeditated. It was merely an intuitive shot in the dark, which had obviously hit a vulnerable spot. He said nothing, wanting her to shape the next moments in their meeting.

Lise, too, was silent for a time, which seemed like an eternity to Lane though it was scarcely more than a minute. Then she said quietly, her voice a bit unsteady, "If you mean, how are things between me and my parents, they aren't going well at all. My father was on the campus this week for a Board meeting, and we spent an unpleasant hour together. He's very critical of my interest in Comparative Literature. Says I'll never make a living with that kind of a major. That I ought to be in Education, or in Business Administration. He wouldn't even be satisfied if my interest in ideas led me to graduate work in theology. He takes a very dim view of women in the clergy."

"What does your mother think?" Lane asked.

"She'll never take issue with him," said Lise. "That's the way she's held things together all these years—by echoing his views, giving in to whatever he wants. I don't even know whether she's a person in her own right. If she is, I've never seen it.

"Dr. Thomas," Lise looked at him directly, not caring that her eyes were still moist, "I don't want to turn out that way. I don't want to live life on my father's terms. Recently my meetings with him have left me very angry, though I've never been able to express that to him. I don't know whether or not I can ever forgive him for what I think he's done to my mother, for what I think he's trying to do to me. I don't know whether or not I can forgive her for letting it happen to her, and to me.

"At the same time, I love my father—at least I think I do. I know he's achieved some important things in his life, and that he's a significant person in the lives of many people in his congregation. And I do respect all of that. But I want to know who I am. I am willing to be his daughter, but I will not be his clone."

Lane Thomas was surprised by her sudden rush of candor. Who could have guessed that his spontaneous question would have so revealing an effect. He should learn to depend less on his habit of linear thinking and to trust his intuition more, he told himself.

He said quietly to Lise, "That hour with your father must have been disappointing and painful. It probably doesn't help a lot for me to tell you that what happened between you and him isn't at all uncommon, but that's true nonetheless. I suspect you may already know it from conversations with your friends.

"The task each of us has—yours and mine—is to become fully ourselves, not spiting what others have given us, but not settling for it passively, either. It's not worth keeping unless we can make it well and truly our own. And sometimes the experience of becoming fully ourselves is wrenching, the more so when it involves saying No to someone we love, or at least someone we respect.

"But when there really is love between two people—between a father and a daughter—then the reciprocal of that love must be a willingness to accept a No without breaking the relationship.

"I suspect it's too early to say whether or not your father was able to hear you clearly. You probably shouldn't make assumptions from his initial response to what you told him. After all, by your account he's not accustomed to people saying No to him. I suggest you give him a little time. And meanwhile, you can continue to work at your own values and goals, the better to tell him who you are even more clearly the next time.

"If I can be of any help in that process," Lane concluded, "don't hesitate to let me know."

Lise had offered her hand in gratitude and left without saying anything more.

That's the way it had begun weeks earlier in the term. And now here she was, the only student in the class who had waited for him forgivingly, in spite of the lateness of his arrival.

His feelings were in a muddle, partly self-conscious embarrassment, partly warmed by her presence. All he could think to say, inanely, was, "Imagine meeting you here!"

CHAPTER THREE
A BAD DAY GETS WORSE

Lane Thomas dreaded the prospect of delivering his tenure dossier in person to Ralph Dwight, chairman of the Religion Department. To have sent it through campus mail would have seemed like deliberate avoidance, not to say a rude affront, since their offices were no more than fifty feet apart.

More than that, the interview was a standard part of the tenure procedure, since a chairman's formal endorsement was required before the faculty Committee on Promotion and Tenure could consider a teacher's tenure application.

So there was no help for it, and it had to be done today, Friday, since the deadline for transmission of the dossier to the Committee was Monday. Lane had requested an appointment with Dwight for three o'clock.

Why did he dread the encounter so? In point of fact, Ralph Dwight had so far left Lane pretty much to himself, had not objected to his course syllabi, even though the bibliographies and course topics suggested an unconventional treatment of theological issues. Lane's primary aim had been to awaken among his students an active curiosity about the subject-matter at hand, as he thought any good undergraduate teacher should do. But the clear implication of this newer Macauley regime was that, in religion especially, "orthodox" adherence ought to be the aim, which offended Lane's evangelical conviction that persuasion was the work of the Holy Spirit.

In spite of their substantial differences in teaching content and style, Ralph Dwight had been quite proper, even cordial, in his personal relationship with Lane. Until now, at least, the Chairman had not brought Lane's nontraditional courses to the attention of the Trustees' Academic Affairs Committee. A part of Dwight's conservative philosophy had been to "let sleeping dogmas lie."

Still Lane was uncomfortable in Dwight's presence. It had something to do with Dwight's graduate background at Fuller Theological Seminary, where he had taken a doctorate in the psychology of religion and where he had taught for a time after receiving the degree. Over a period of years, Fuller had moved from its initial orientation—it was founded in 1947 by the long-time radio evangelist Charles E. Fuller and some other prominent fundamentalists—to its present, far broader and more open evangelical stance, to the great distress of fundamentalists who were now its most vocal detractors. But Ralph Dwight had studied there before that transition was fully accomplished, and Lane felt in Dwight more than a remnant of Fuller's earlier fundamentalist tradition— felt it as much in the Chairman's vocal inflections and in a rhetorical style that seemed always on the verge of issuing an altar call.

More than that, Lane and everybody else knew that Dwight had been picked for his position by President Kean to be the point-man for the college's aggressive new religious conservatism. While Dwight would move cautiously, not wanting to stir controversy within the college nor to draw the attention of the American Association of University Professors to questionable academic decisions, Lane Thomas wondered how long it would be before Ralph Dwight would find some plausible reason for ridding the college of this closet theological "liberal" in its midst.

And when better to do it than when a routine tenure decision was being made. There are all kinds of grounds for denying tenure, and they are not necessarily the ones that are publicly announced.

So when Lane Thomas approached the chairman's office door as the Chapel bells chimed three across the campus, it was with considerable foreboding and a fervent wish that the interview be over as quickly and painlessly as possible.

Ralph Dwight greeted him cordially enough and motioned him to a settee. Dwight was twenty years Lane's senior, tall but slight of frame, hair decidedly thinning, and the granny-glasses he effected gave him a slightly spinsterish look that was reinforced by rather fussy mannerisms. The top of his desk was entirely free of books and papers, and the orderliness that marked the rest of the room was in stark contrast to the apparent chaos that invaded most faculty offices on this campus.

Dwight came out from behind his desk and sat in a straight chair beside the settee, obviously wanting—but not quite managing—to create an air of informality in their meeting.

"Things going well with you this term?" Dwight asked with his usual tight smile.

"Yes. Well, I think so," Lane replied, without great assurance. And then conscious of his tentative sound he added, "The students seem to be applying themselves with reasonable seriousness. Some of them are doing really quite well, and I have spent as much out-of-class time with them as possible to encourage their work. Of course, putting together this tenure dossier has been a major preoccupation"—he handed the large, loose-leaf binder to Dwight as he spoke—"and with this done, I'll have more time now for contact with students. I consider it indispensable to good teaching."

"I wish more of our colleagues took that view," Dwight replied approvingly. "I recall what a difference that kind of special encouragement made to my own enthusiasm for undergraduate learning at Westmont College.

"By the way," the Chairman added, "do you know who Lise Warner is? I think she's enrolled in one of your Christian Thought courses."

"Yes," Lane admitted, conscious that he may have colored a bit at Dwight's question and feeling as if he had been found out—though of what he didn't know. "Yes, Lise is a very bright student. She's majoring in Comparative Literature, as I understand it, and my course on 'Theological Issues in Contemporary Literature' is a natural for her. I suppose the fact that, as a Preacher's Kid, she has more than the average background on the religion side also adds to the rightness of the match. In any event, she's enthusiastic and attentive. Why do you ask?"

"As you probably know," said Ralph Dwight, "her father is the senior minister of Judson-First Baptist Church in Capital City, the largest of our supporting congregations. He was elected last spring to Macauley's Board of Trustees and was quickly chosen to fill the vacancy left by the unexpected death of the previous Chairman a short time before. He's obviously somebody we want to cultivate carefully, so it's important that his daughter has a good experience here at Macauley. I'm sure you understand. No special considerations, of course, but—a word to the wise."

Lane found the implications of Dwight's "word to the wise" troubling, but he made no response.

What followed was pretty routine. Ralph Dwight talked about Lane's course load, reviewed his largely favorable student evaluations, looked over his service on the Library Committee and on the Student Religious Activities Board, and noted for the record Lane's membership in nearby All Soul's Church (Episcopal)—local-church membership being, for all practical purposes, required to demonstrate "good faith"—the irony was not lost on Lane—by teachers in the Religion Department.

"Oh, by the way," said Dwight, as if in casual afterthought, "I've learned in recent weeks through the local media that you folks at All Souls have called a lesbian as your new associate rector. Do I remember correctly that you were on the Search Committee?"

Lane felt his face flush. Was he more uncomfortable with the gay-lesbian issue than he had admitted to himself, especially when it related to clergy ordination and pastoral leadership? Or was he discomfited by Dwight's question because he sensed that it might be the beginning of the inquiry into his personal view of ethics and theology that he had been dreading?

Lane felt pretty sure that his case for tenure and a permanent appointment at Macauley College was strong on formal academic grounds. Except for the indifferent crowd in his current theology and literature course, his teaching had been generally well-regarded by students, and he had managed to publish several journal articles, one or two of them greeted as quite original in pursuit of his interest in what he called "a theological aesthetic." But given the new conservative image being fashioned for Macauley by President Kean and his hand-picked Trustees, Lane was much less sure that his personal views, however evangelical, would stand up favorably under more conservative scrutiny.

Come to that, why would he even want a permanent appointment at Macauley in the presence of such an increasingly single-minded and uncongenial regime? Unfortunately, the answer was simple. Academic positions, especially in the field of religious studies, weren't easy to find in these retrenching times. One did better to hold on to what one had as long as one could. Even if it were not to one's preferred taste, a bird in the hand at least offered some nourishment, especially if there were none to be had in the bush.

"Yes," Lane managed to acknowledge with a calmness that belied his apprehension, "I was one of twelve members on the committee, and it was quite an educational experience. We conducted a national search, received more than 50 applications, and the whole process took us far longer than anyone anticipated. I suppose if I had known at the beginning that we would just be finishing our work a year later, I might have declined the appointment.

"But it was worth the time it took. We got an insight into the state of the ministry in mainline churches that we probably couldn't have gotten in any other way."

"And what did you learn?" Ralph Dwight wanted to know. Lane wished that he hadn't virtually invited that further question by the way he had framed his response. The last thing he wanted to do was to prolong a discussion with Dwight about the recent controversial decision made by his church—a decision he knew would not have been looked on favorably by the college authorities. But now there was no help for it.

"One of the things we learned," said Lane, "was how many really talented people there are, women as well as men, in the job market.

We learned, too, that denominationalism is in trouble these days. I knew that denominational affiliations tend to be treated rather casually by lay folks and that their denominational loyalties are not very deep, but I didn't realize the extent to which that's true for the clergy too. We actually had a several applications from people whose ordinations were outside of the Episcopal Church. Denominations are going to have to redefine themselves in the next decade—reshape their identity and mission."

All that seemed reasonably unprovocative, Lane thought, hoping it would deflect any deeper probing by the Chairman. But he was not to be delivered so easily from a further discussion of the lesbian appointment.

"Were there other homosexual candidates in what you describe as a large and talented pool?" Dwight wanted to know. So, the dreaded inquisition was under way, and there was no way now to dodge it.

In fact, Lane thought, why should he even want to avoid it. Better to step directly into it, get it behind him, let it do whatever it would do. It's not as if he had done anything reprehensible, however appalling the decision in which he had participated might seem to President Kean and Dwight and the conservative Trustees.

In fact, he was quite proud of the committee's recommendation and of the parish's overwhelming vote in support of it. Better, perhaps, to take a positive, even aggressive stance, as if the college should have no reason to question what he had done as a Search Committee member.

"As a matter of fact, there were several who identified themselves quite openly as homosexual," Lane replied with new conviction. "And there were two or three others where we caught the implication—where there may not have been quite the courage to declare themselves openly.

"That reluctance is hardly surprising," Lane went on, now increasingly sure of himself. "Some of the declared ones have had nothing but disappointment from other search committees that repeatedly refused even to consider their candidacies. And when one of them was given consideration and invited to make a candidate visit to a church, he met unbelievable insensitivity and even cruelty at the hands of a supposedly Christian congregation and, in the end, was rejected. It was all quite shocking," Lane added firmly.

"Tell me, was the recommendation from the Search Committee to your congregation unanimous?" Ralph Dwight pressed, indirectly but without subtlety.

"It was," Lane declared. "All twelve of us were agreed that Sandra Albright was the most qualified candidate among the 50 we had considered. We weren't out to make a statement, whether politically correct or politically incorrect. We simply believed that her personal and professional strengths best matched the leadership needs our parish had identified. Given that, in our view her homosexuality was irrelevant."

"So that is your view as well, is it?" Dwight persisted. His voice raised at the end of the sentence, as if asking a question, but it was, in fact, a statement. Although said quietly, to Lane it had the sound of an accusation.

"Yes, that is my view," said Lane deliberately, now calm and fully engaged, heedless for the moment of the implications his responses might have for the tenure decision. "At least, it became my view the more I studied and thought about it during the course of the search"

He decided to meet his Chairman's implied accusation head on. "Of course, I've read the biblical references to homosexuality carefully, and it just doesn't seem to me that they justify the enormous furor some Christians have generated around them.

"What impresses me is how relatively little attention is given to the issue, both in the Hebrew scriptures and in the Christian writings," Lane went on, feeling now that he was on a roll. "There is the prohibition in Leviticus 18:20, and the call for the death penalty in 20:13. There is a passing reference to homosexuality by Paul in Romans 1. And whoever wrote I Timothy—probably not Paul—included it in a list of 'lawless and disobedient' acts in the epistle's first chapter.

"There's no reference to female homosexuality anywhere in the Hebrew scriptures, and the only one in the New Testament is in Paul's list of `degrading passions' in Romans 1."

Suddenly sensing that all this might sound condescending, as if he thought Ralph Dwight needed instructing on the subject, Lane stopped and said, somewhat apologetically, "I realize you know all of this. But since you seemed to want to know on what basis I was able to participate, in good conscience, in the recommendation made to the parish by the Search Committee, I thought I should fill you in as fully as possible.

"And there was one more consideration," Lane quickly added, without giving Dwight a chance to get back into the conversation. "There is no reference to homosexuality anywhere in the Gospels. In fact, the chief burden of Jesus' ministry was to challenge the prevailing 'politics of purity' that was current in the religious community of his time, and to replace it with the 'politics of compassion,' as one New Testament scholar recently put it.

"The prohibition against male homosexuality in Leviticus was only one small detail in an enormous, elaborated 'purity system' that was presumed to make us acceptable to a God with a cleanliness compulsion. Jesus opposed that system. He said that only what came out of the human heart could make us clean or unclean, and that what made us acceptable to God was not some supposed external purity but a life of compassion.

"So I agree with that biblical scholar: when Paul summarized the Christian message, saying that 'In Christ there is neither Jew nor Gentile, male nor female, slave nor free,' he could as well have added, 'neither gay nor straight.'"

"As you probably know, the Bishop of our diocese, in company with a great others throughout the church, has determined that homosexuality is not a bar to ordination and the practice of ministry."

After that rush of what had become an increasingly passionate statement the longer it ran on, Ralph Dwight was silent for a few moments. Then he said, "I find that an astonishing conclusion for one who denominates himself an evangelical. I take it you've been reading the stuff produced by some of those people in the Jesus Seminar."

The Seminar was a group of biblical scholars, formed in 1987, that met twice a year to vote on the likelihood that a given passage in the Gospels was, or wasn't, an authentic saying of Jesus. And because the Seminar repudiated the notion of a divine authority that inhered uniformly and without exception in the whole of the Old and New Testaments, it had infuriated many on the theological right wing. The fact that Dwight referred to the products of the Jesus Seminar as "stuff" clearly signaled his view of the enterprise.

"I should have thought," Dwight said, "that as a sound teacher of religious studies, you might have sought guidance from a source that had more regard for the integrity of Scripture."

Lane, caught up in the momentum of his recital, was unprepared for this rebuke. He could only stammer in response, "But I thought—it seemed to me—that is, as I read their intent, the purpose of the Jesus Seminar is precisely to confirm the integrity of Scripture—to determine where its real authority lies."

"We shall have to continue this discussion at another time, since I'm due at a committee meeting in ten minutes," said Dwight dismissively, clearly not interested in setting a time for such continuance.

"Well, thank you for hearing me out," said Lane. And then wanting to end the conversation on an anticipatory note, he added, "I really do enjoy my teaching here and I hope to be able to continue it for the foreseeable future."

"Yes. Well," said Dwight without rising to Lane's bait, and signaling the end to the interview, "I'll probably see you later this afternoon at the faculty meeting."

They shook hands, and Lane walked out of the Chairman's office, down the stairs, and out onto the late-autumn campus. Its colors were fading, and its air was sharp.

CHAPTER FOUR

A WELCOME INTERLUDE

After his draining encounter with Ralph Dwight, Lane felt the need for a strong, restorative cup of coffee, and he headed for the Campus Union to get it.

There, sitting at a table by herself, was Dr. Anne Armstrong, Associate Professor of Political Science, and Lane's sometime social companion. Anne, a brilliant student, had earned her Ph.D. by age 22 and had been tenured two years ago at an age—28—when most academics are still struggling to establish themselves. She had been a member of the faculty search committee that brought Lane to Macauley, and he had been impressed by her from the start. Anne was no more than 5'4" tall, slimly proportioned, and had the fresh good looks of a coed ten years younger for whom she was regularly mistaken. Physically and intellectually energetic, Anne was always a step ahead of Lane in both spheres and, while he had first found that energy a bit off-putting, in time respect for her had turned to genuine affection.

Were they dating, or just doing things together? Lane had recently had a hard time trying to figure that out. Early in their relationship—fully a year ago—Anne had set the boundaries pretty firmly. They had had several dates—at least as Lane considered them—and one day, after spending an hour jogging together, Anne suddenly said to him at a rest stop, "Do you have a romantic interest in me?"

Lane was startled by the suddenness and directness of her question. He couldn't tell from the form of the question what kind of answer might be acceptable to her, and in any case he didn't have time to calculate his response. So all he could do was reply with an ingenuous "Yes."

"Well, don't have!" Anne had said, and took off again down the jogging path ahead of him.

So Lane had put off his aspiration for a more serious, more intimate relationship with Anne, and had simply decided to content himself, at least for the foreseeable future, with the pleasure of her company, which he found very pleasant indeed, on its—actually on her—own terms.

More recently Lane had tried to determine whether or not there had been any change in their relationship, but Anne hadn't been particularly forthcoming. Which probably meant that she still didn't take it all that seriously. At least, not seriously enough to move it to a more intimate level, but too seriously to give it up.

Having recently gone through the tenure process herself, Anne had been particularly helpful to Lane in determining what he could most usefully include in his dossier. Of course, the faculty Committee on Promotion and Tenure had supplied formal guidelines and a model dossier table of contents, but the question of how to weight the various suggested elements was left pretty much to the candidate and whatever advice he could get from people who had been through it before him.

Anne had been generous with her time and advice, and Lane was sure his dossier was stronger as a result of her counsel.

She smiled a warm greeting as he approached, coffee in hand from the self-service counter. "So, did you turn in the *magnum opus* this afternoon?" she asked. Lane nodded as he swigged a grateful draft from his cup.

"How did the interview go with Ralph Dwight?" she wanted to know.

"It was the interview from hell," Lane said as he collapsed into the booth beside her. He told her about Dwight's initially subtle, then more direct probing into how fully Lane had shared in, and therefore had shared responsibility for, the recommendation to call a lesbian to the ministry of All Souls.

"Once I got into it, I realized that I didn't really want to dodge the issue. I was sure that Dwight wouldn't approve, of course. I've suspected for some time that underneath his laid-back, apparently accepting manner, he's really a theological redneck. Now there's no doubt about it. He virtually sneered at the idea that gays and lesbians might be included in the love of God. Why should I give in to that kind of homophobic bigotry? Why should I be expected to act as if I'm the one who has something to explain, that I'm the one who has stepped outside of the circle of faith?"

Clearly, the emotional rush Lane had felt as he warmed to his subject in Dwight's office hadn't been entirely cooled by the autumn chill of his walk from Founders Hall to the Union.

Anne was astonished by a level of intensity and conviction she hadn't seen in Lane before. One reason for her past lack of real enthusiasm for their relationship had been a sense that, while he was obviously very bright and pleasant enough as an occasional companion, he was a bit too agreeable, his views a bit too malleable. In short, she thought he lacked definition. Now she reflected that perhaps there really was more to him than she had guessed.

But now Lane was momentarily uncertain. "Did I do the right thing, do you think?" he asked anxiously.

"Of course you did the right thing," Anne responded at once, wanting to reinforce this new evidence of ego-strength in him.

"And I'm proud of you for doing it. Morally it was the only thing you could do. Politically—well, that's something else again. It's possible that Dwight and President Kean will hold it against you in their tenure decision. But what you do with your private life away from the campus ought to have no bearing whatever on decisions they make about you here."

Anne went on. "Short of some egregious act of 'moral turpitude'—as you well know, that's the standard term that has been used in faculty handbooks everywhere to define grounds for summary dismissal, even for termination of tenure—things like robbing a bank, or trying to seduce the mayor's wife, or being caught with your pants down in City Park—short of that kind of thing, what you do in your private life is simply none of their business.

And any effort to intrude themselves is just an effort at arbitrary administrative intimidation."

"Speaking of power politics," said Lane, "something else came up in my meeting with Dwight. He tried to put the bite on me in relation to a student in one of my classes. He asked me if I knew Lise Warner. I do, of course. I'm sure he knew that before he asked. He made a point of reminding me that her father, a recent appointee to the Board of Trustees, is the Board's new Chairman.

"He was clearly warning me that, unless Lise has a good experience at Macauley—which obviously includes her experience in my class—the Reverend Dr. John Warner could become a serious problem to the college, which of course means that he could become a really serious problem for me. I think he was telling me that my future in Macauley College may very well depend on how I'm regarded by John Warner."

"So what's the prospect?" asked Anne. "I mean, how is Lise doing in the class? What's her attitude toward the work, toward you?"

"All very positive," said Lane. "She's easily the best student in the class. She's majoring in Comparative Literature, has obviously read widely even before coming to college. In the rather suffocating atmosphere of the family, it must have been her way out into a larger world. Little did her parents suspect that her reading was more subversive than a less restrictive life-style would have been. As a consequence, she has a remarkable facility with language, In fact, she's written by far the best crafted and most thoughtful papers I've ever received from a student.

"More than that, I've spent time with her around some personal issues, so our relationship is solid. I can tell you, quite confidentially, that I'm not the only one for whom the Reverend John Warner could spell trouble. He already spells trouble for his daughter."

Anne stood up and reached for her coat, obviously intent on leaving. "Wait," said Lane. "Don't go yet. Do you have an appointment?"

"Yes," said Anne, "and so do you. Have you forgotten the faculty meeting at 4:30?"

Lane groaned as he got up to go. "What a thoroughly unsatisfactory way," he said, "to end a thoroughly unsatisfactory day!"

CHAPTER FIVE

A STARTLING ANNOUNCEMENT

Lane dreaded faculty meetings. He enjoyed his faculty colleagues when he met them one by one, but when they came together to consider the business of the college, they seemed to undergo a character change. Women and men who were individually civil, even generous and compassionate, suddenly became carping and contentious, suspicious that there was a plot under every proposal if only it could be ferreted out and exposed.

Whenever Lane thought about faculty meetings, he recalled theologian Reinhold Niebuhr's 1932 book on *Moral Man and Immoral Society*. The contrast in that title certainly fit his experience as an individual in this academic collective. Niebuhr had written that

> *Individual men may be moral in the sense that they are able to consider interests other than their own in determining problems of conduct, and are capable, on occasion, of preferring the advantages of others to their own. They are endowed by nature with a measure of sympathy and consideration for their kind....But all these achievements are more difficult, if not impossible, for human societies and social groups. In every human group there is less reason to guide and check impulse, less capacity for self-transcendence, less ability to comprehend the needs of others and therefore more unrestrained egoism than the individuals, who compose the group, reveal in their personal relationships.*

Amen! Lane thought. This faculty group was at its carping, nitpicking worst on issues that mattered least to the character and quality of the college, which seemed like a further confirmation of Niebuhr. A proposed new course, even an entire new program, could be approved without a murmur; but introduce a change in the method by which faculty mail was to be distributed, and the arguing was interminable.

Lane could understand how some cynic had once defined a college faculty as a group of men and women held together by a common grievance against parking.

And in spite of the length of the arguments, nothing ever seemed to get permanently settled in faculty meetings. What had apparently been decided in one session had to be decided all over again at the next. Although as a faculty person he had resented the characterization when he first heard it, he had to admit there was some truth in it: a faculty meeting, somebody had said, resembles nothing so much as a bunch of little birds trying to build a nest in a big wind.

The element of suspicion, even of paranoia, that seemed so often in or just under the surface of faculty meeting discussions, may have come out of the collective disposition Reinhold Niebuhr had written about. But it certainly was not helped by a president who seemed never able to express himself clearly and unequivocally. That described Charles Kean to a fault. The general assumption academics make about their presidents is that, if they are bright enough to hold that office, they are also bright enough to think, and hence to speak, clearly—that is, comprehendingly and comprehensively—about institutional purposes and policies. And if they do not, in fact, speak thus clearly, they must surely be up to something!

A distinguished Washington correspondent during the Eisenhower years had once insisted that Ike's cloudy rhetoric and circumlocutions in press conferences were not the product of a fuzzy mind but of a clever one. They were a calculated instrument of political flexibility, permitting him to avoid public commitments that later might have to be altered.

With Charles Kean, it was difficult to tell whether his flawed rhetoric was the result of calculation or confusion. His public discourse was usually filled with triteness and with sentences that doubled back upon themselves. In fact, at the annual student talent show, which was always an occasion for taking off members of the faculty and administration, a student who portrayed President Kean giving a typical campus speech had brought down the house when he said, "I am not redundant, and besides I do not repeat myself!"

All of these reflections added to Lane's glumness and apprehension as he and Anne arrived at the Library Conference Room, where monthly faculty meetings were held. By long-standing agreement, they took seats in different parts of the room. Since it was common knowledge that they had a special friendship, they didn't want to give anyone the impression, by sitting together, that they might constitute a voting bloc.

As he often did, Lane sat down beside Jim Denison, long-time professor of philosophy in Macauley College, an irreverent Roman Catholic and an equally irreverent observer of the foibles of faculty and administration alike. Lane liked to sit next to Jim because sometimes the only relief from the crashing boredom of this monthly event was an often hilarious comment on the proceedings, discreetly whispered to Lane from behind Denison's hand.

Lane's odds-on favorite whispered comment was the time Li Chang, professor of physics, had accomplished some particularly deft parliamentary maneuver in behalf of one of his favorite academic interests. Jim Denison whispered to Lane, "It seems to me that I detect the fine Italian hand of the inscrutable Asiatic!"

The only hope Lane held out for this particular faculty meeting was that it might result in a reprise from Jim Denison. Otherwise it was likely to be eminently forgettable.

President Kean gaveled for attention and asked Professor Ralph Dwight to offer an invocation. As usual, Dwight did something odd to his voice when intoning a public prayer. His inflections seemed to suggest the roar of the greasepaint (or at any rate of the sawdust) and the smell of the crowd. Often, on such occasions, he instructed God at some length. This time, at least, his instruction was blessedly brief.

A motion to approve the Minutes of last month's meeting as

distributed was adopted by voice vote of the two or three who bothered to respond to the "All in favor say, aye" invitation. Of course, no one accepted the "Those opposed, by a like sign" invitation. Probably no more than two or three of the 50 or so present had even read the Minutes.

The meeting agenda was filled with committee reports and announcements, none of which required any action and all of which could have been communicated more effectively in writing, without the nearly 50 person-hours this gathering was wasting. By now the time was approaching 5:30, and there was a palpable restlessness in the room as the gathering anticipated adjournment and escape out into the bracing fall air.

But President Kean wasn't ready to gavel the meeting to a close. He had one more item to present for the faculty's information. He wanted to announce a policy decision made by the Board of Trustees at its recent meeting, he said. Since that decision was within the Board's prerogative, it did not require ratification by the faculty, but he expressed the expectation that the faculty would, of course, give the new policy its full support.

He proceeded to explain. "All of us who live and work with college-age young people these days know that these are pretty confusing times for them." Then he said the same thing in two or three different ways, and faculty auditors groaned inwardly as they anticipated another vintage Charles Kean performance that could go well past 5:30 and, at whatever length, was unlikely to land on anything substantive. They settled in, once more, for the long haul.

Kean went on. "If this college is to be worth its salt, if it is serious about its educational mission, if it cares about the characters and the eternal destinies of its students, and if it intends to reassure parents about the moral safety of the sons and daughters they have entrusted to us"—everywhere faculty heads were nodding now, lulled by the President's drone and the late afternoon warmth of the room—"we must set a clear standard, offer an example of principled living, point the direction to moral health."

He paused, presumably for a dramatic effect that was lost on the soporific assembly. Then he went on. "The policy that I am announcing today is designed to set such a standard. I am pleased to say that, while I called the issue to the Board's attention, it was enthusiastically endorsed by the Board's chairman, the Reverend Dr. John Warner, as a step in bringing our campus practice into line with our Christian profession. The new policy was adopted unanimously by those Trustees present and will immediately become an amendment to our handbook statement on 'Student Conduct at Macauley College.' I ask each of you to give it your active support and to assist in its implementation."

Kean came to the point. "The Board has determined that homosexuality in students, whether actively practiced or merely acknowledged, shall be grounds for immediate dismissal from the College, with prejudice and without appeal. Announcement of this new policy will be made by Dr. Warner at an on-campus press conference this coming Friday, one week from today. Until then, I want it understood that the information is not to go beyond this room."

Now the assemblage was fully awake, even before Kean's adjourning gavel struck the podium with an exclamatory report.

There was a sharp, audible intake of breath from Jim Denison. Too startled to whisper, his words came out with a hiss.

"JesusMaryandJoseph!" was all he was able to say.

SATURDAY

CHAPTER SIX
A GATHERING CRISIS

It was very like President Charles Kean to wait until the very last minute in a late Friday afternoon faculty meeting to announce something he thought might be controversial.

That way the announcement, preceded by the numbing desensitization of an invariably boring agenda, was inserted at a moment when everyone was intent on ending the meeting as soon as possible in order to hurry home to supper, the quicker to inaugurate the weekend.

Under that circumstance, there was less tendency for teachers to stand around after the meeting and engage in the mutual reinforcement of any prospective grievances the announcement might have aroused. And there was less likelihood that organized opposition might begin to form on the spot out of individual discontent.

Then with weekend distractions intervening, discontent tended to dissipate somewhat by the time they were on campus again on Monday. The President's method was far from foolproof, but it had served him admirably on more than one occasion.

This wasn't one of them.

There wasn't much standing around on Friday afternoon after Kean made the announcement from the Board of Trustees about student homosexuality, but the issue was by no means ignored. Appalled as Lane Thomas and Jim Denison were, they didn't part after the meeting and hurry home to their suppers until they had made a fervent agreement to talk the next morning.

It was scarcely after eight o'clock when Denison rang up Lane and launched at once upon a trajectory of outrage that had become more elevated the more he had thought about it.

"It seems to me that it's awfully late in the day, as human history is measured, to be perpetrating this kind of red-neck homophobia,"

Denison began. "I expect it in my local parish, mired as this particular diocese is in the anti-modern views of the Roman Curia. I don't like it any better there, but at least I expect it from a bishop who thinks the present Pope is infallible whether he is speaking *ex cathedra* or not.

"On the other hand," Denison went on, warming to his subject, "I suppose Charlie Kean is like the Pope. Charlie thinks God has made him infallible, too."

Ordinarily President Kean was called "Charles" by those few senior members of the faculty who felt free to approach him with some degree of informality, and "Charles" was what he called himself. Jim Denison referred to Kean privately, and with derogatory intent, as "Charlie" whenever he was inclined to be critical of some presidential behavior—which was, in fact, most of the time.

"But this isn't the Vatican," Jim Denison went on without skipping a beat. "And it isn't St. Monica's Parish. It's a bleeding liberal arts college! My God, one ought to expect something more enlightened from an institution that professes to have its roots in a humane tradition."

In the face of Denison's verbal momentum, Lane Thomas was reduced to making confirmatory noises on his end of the telephone line.

Denison persisted. "Charlie Kean himself is always saying, in some convocation or other, that one of the purposes of an undergraduate liberal arts education is to help students arrive at a clearer sense of self. And he's right about that, of course. What better outcome from four years of intellectual and personal exploration than to come away from it knowing authentically who you are? As a philosopher, there is no doubt in my mind that reliable self-knowledge is the most precious kind. Maybe also the rarest.

"But suppose, as a consequence of being a student in this kind of a place, that what you discover authentically is that you are gay? Now Charlie and his Tory Trustees are telling us that we can't permit that kind of authenticity.

"So what are we supposed to tell a gay student? Go be authentic somewhere else? It's a travesty!"

However rhetorical Jim Denison's question was, Lane thought it lay pretty close to the human heart of the matter. He had come to his open view of gays and lesbians rather late. Unequivocally hetero himself, there were no gays among his circle of friends—at least none that he knew of—and there simply had been no particular occasion for him to think much about the matter.

That ended a year ago when he was appointed to the Search Committee at All Souls Church and had been confronted with the impressive application of Sandra Albright for the Associate Rector position. At that point he had read as widely as he could, both psychological and theological tracts on the subject, and concluded that gays and lesbians should be welcomed as full members both of the body politic and the body ecclesiastic. Getting to know Sandra Albright since her arrival had fully confirmed him in that view.

When Jim Denison paused for breath, Lane got into the discussion. "I agree," he said. "To repress one's true self voluntarily is dangerous. To be required to repress one's true self is likely to be disastrous."

"Precisely," said Denison. "In fact, I'm surprised we haven't had a student suicide already. This latest stupidity by Charlie Kean and the Board will certainly increase the likelihood."

He went on, his voice now quiet but intense. "I've been concerned for some weeks, because the atmosphere among students on the campus seems to me to be tacitly but decisively homophobic. There hasn't been much talk about the issue, and that may be evidence that hostility does lie just beneath the surface. Talk about gays is certainly prominent enough in public discourse—about their participation in the military, about their eligibility to hold elective office. Why don't our students talk about it? It's almost as if there has been an unspoken agreement among them to keep the issue hidden for fear that it couldn't be controlled if once it were to break through. The whole thing is entirely mindless. It's not as if they had thought about it, and certainly not that they know anything about it. It's merely an attitude they have brought with them from home.

"And this latest idiocy will simply endorse their redneck inclinations, give students a good conscience about their latent hostility, maybe even bring it to the surface."

"Unfortunately I can confirm your impression," said Lane. "Some months ago, when we discussed Sandra Albright's application in our Search Committee, we raised a question about how acceptable a lesbian minister would be to Macauley students. The student representative on the Committee, though supportive of Sandra's application, warned us that there might be a problem in campus relationships. We considered it carefully and, since Sandra was clearly the ablest candidate we had, we determined not to be intimidated by that possibility. Fortunately, the members of the parish concurred."

Since both Jim Denison and Lane Thomas had other colleagues they wanted to talk with, and since this call had confirmed what they were sure would be the case—that they were in total agreement on the potential disaster the Trustees were perpetrating—they concluded their conversation with a promise to confer again when they were both on the campus on Monday.

Once his line was free, Lane tried to call Anne Armstrong, but he got a busy signal for the better part of an hour. When he finally reached her in mid-morning, he found that she had been trying to reach him while he was on the line with Jim Denison, and in the meantime she had called some of her own departmental colleagues.

Anne's take on the issue of the Trustees' policy decision was different from Jim's and Lane's, though no less negative. Not that she found the content of the Trustees' policy any more acceptable than Jim and Lane did; but in contrast to those two who taught philosophy and religious studies, Anne as a political scientist was concerned about what she viewed as the procedural outrage of what the Trustees were proposing to do.

She and her fellow political scientists were agreed, she told Lane, that whether or not the Trustees had the authority to act, unilaterally and without faculty consultation, on policy affecting so-called 'student affairs' was a bit cloudy. But there was no such cloud when it came to educational policy, where the Handbook clearly gave initiative to the faculty—though always subject to Trustee review.

"Have you looked recently at the section of the Macauley catalog that deals with the purpose of the institution?" Anne asked Lane. "It's up there near the front. You may never have looked at it. Most faculty members haven't, but it's there in black and white anyway. And guess what," said Anne. "There are three quotations from other educators, cited as examples of the Macauley view of undergraduate learning. Here's one of them." She read:

> ...the liberal arts are not subjects in the curriculum. Rather, they are personal qualities—the attributes of men and women that enlarge their capacity for uncoerced choice.

Here's another," she said:

> Liberal education has as its aim the fullest possible development of the individual personality.

"And here's the third." Again she read:

> The aim of the liberal arts education is to make men and women more fully human. The whole person is to be educated and human wholeness is the end of liberal education.

"And then," said Anne, "the catalog says, 'Macauley College stands with these classic definitions of educational purpose and intends to embody them.' That statement probably antedates the current administration. It sounds more like Dean Morton Emmons. But there it is, whoever put it there. It stands as the official specification—the contractual stipulation, if you will—to which this place is committed."

"Am I getting through to you at all?" Anne asked when Lane wasn't very responsive.

"Spell it out to me, just in case," Lane pleaded.

"Based on this," Anne explained, "a case can be made that the Board exceeded its authority when it acted unilaterally on its anti-homosexual policy. It's true that there is no specific provision in the Handbook on faculty involvement in so-called 'student affairs' policy. But that's only because, in this kind of a college, the learning that arises out of 'student affairs' isn't distinguished from other kinds of learning. One of the distinctive things about this place, and others like it, is that personal growth, personal development, personal learning in students are as much a part of the college's educational mission as classroom courses are.

"That means all of it is really educational policy, and on that the Handbook is clear: that's the faculty's job."

"It also means," said Anne with a note of triumph in her voice, "that the Trustees may have screwed up on this one!"

SUNDAY

CHAPTER SEVEN
AN UNUSUAL SUNDAY

It wasn't Lise Warner's habit to attend church on Sunday mornings during Macauley College's academic year.

Earlier in her life, of course, church attendance had been unexceptionable: a family requirement and hence never questioned. The requirement included not only the 11 o'clock service every Sunday morning, but also the Baptist Youth Fellowship every Sunday night, and, until she was able to beg off in her later high school years on the excuse of having to study in order to keep up an academic average that would get her into college, Prayer and Bible Study Meetings every Wednesday night. On annual occasions when there was a week-long crusade conducted by a visiting evangelist, Lise went uncomplainingly but unenthusiastically every night.

Since her father usually conducted the services, she was ordinarily expected to sit with her mother, Ellen. If you had asked Lise, back then, how she felt about her father always being center-stage in these events, she would have seemed not to understand the question. After all, she had never known it any other way.

If you were to ask her now, she would tell you that "center-stage" was ironically precise. Over time the conclusion had gradually awakened in her that the Reverend John Warner was without profound religious experience, that he was playing a role as spiritual leader and was very good at it, that he fed on the adulation that skilled role brought him, and that he had probably never permitted himself to acknowledge, even for a moment, the truth of his own emptiness.

He was certainly not a bad man. Probably he had actually done a great deal of good as a by-product of his role-playing. But he was an inauthentic man. However she had felt inside, Lise could not bring herself to be overtly angry with him. Rather she grieved for his studied inability to be real, and she ached for his false sense of self.

The worst of it, she knew, was that she was like him. She had always been a "good" girl, which meant that she had always been a docile, obedient daughter. At the age of 12, when it was expected that "good" girls and boys from "good" church homes would be baptized, according to the rite of her father's Baptist tradition, Lise conformed. She went through the expected instruction, submitted herself to the expected immersionist ritual, made the expected professions, and accepted the expected congratulations of family and church friends.

What her parents never suspected was the secret life Lise had guarded jealously. Lane had no way of knowing how intuitively right he had been in describing Lise to Anne Armstrong: that her wide reading had given Lise subversive access to another world, one in stark contrast to the ambiance of her daily existence. She was particularly drawn to literary images of strong women, for example in the works of Hendrik Ibsen and Jane Austen, and had even found her way into some of the classic spiritual works of Hildegard of Bingen and Julian of Norwich. She read Alice Walker on her own, and a high school English teacher, sensing Lise's precocity and need, turned her onto Virginia Woolf and Doris Lessing and the poetry of Adrienne Rich. She had been excited—and freed—by the contemporary spirituality of Nancy Mairs' *Ordinary Time*, and her passion to write was strongly shaped by Mairs' *Voice Lessons* and by Anne Lamott's *Bird by Bird*.

Such authors were the primary companions of an otherwise lonely adolescence. She internalized their influences hungrily, made them distinctively her own, aspired to their clarity and strength though often despairing that she could ever achieve the distance needed to draw those qualities out, to make her outer life the shape of her inner. And as a consequence of living deeply within that universe of literary discourse, her own quite unselfconscious articulation had become literate beyond her years.

Externally, during high school Lise conformed to the behavioral expectations of her family. While occasionally she went to social events as part of a mixed group of young people, primarily from her father's church, who sometimes did things together, she yielded to her parents' apprehensions about dating and kept individual young men at a safe and uncontaminating distance. By the time she got to college, the habit of avoiding male companionship had become so strong that she hardly gave dating a thought.

Not that she wasn't attractive—very attractive, as Lane Thomas had come to realize. She had both remarkable physical grace and an alluring "presence" that suggested something deeply mysterious in her—Lane hadn't been able to figure out how else to describe to himself the effect she had on him, and had surely had on others as well. She had simply said No to dating invitations often enough that word got around and pretty soon the invitations stopped.

The person for whom Lise had the strongest feeling, primarily of pity, was her mother, Ellen, whom she saw as the primary victim of her father's emptiness. In her early years, of course, she was quite unaware of anything false in Ellen's life. Oddly enough, a question first insinuated itself in her mind while sitting in church. She began to realize, when she was perhaps 15, that her mother never sang the hymns in the service, though Ellen's speaking voice suggested that she might be a very pleasant alto. Something in her mother's demeanor had always kept Lise from asking her about that. Later Lise realized that her mother never led with prayers in the family or in church meetings, and that she had never heard her mother express a spontaneous religious conviction.

"Shy" was the way her father's parishioners tended to describe Ellen. Lise had come to a different conclusion. There was, she finally sensed, a profound disappointment and sadness in her mother. To the extent that her father had led a false life, Ellen had permitted that same falseness to shape her own existence. She had lived a conforming life, subordinating herself, losing herself, not so much to her husband as to her husband's role.

As is often true with sadness, Lise came to believe that at its base there was, in her mother, great anger. And anger which is inexpressible, which must be suppressed because to express it would be to destroy even what is valued, takes the form of a sadness too deep for sighing.

So, in spite of her usual habit of sleeping in on college Sunday mornings, on this particular Sunday morning Lise found herself approaching the entrance of All Souls Church just prior to the 11 o'clock service. The church was located three blocks from the main part of the campus, between the campus and the town's central business district, so Lise frequently passed the building and would sometimes give casual attention to announcements on its outdoor reader board. Ordinarily a Baptist might well feel uncomfortable on proposing to enter an Episcopal church, so arcane and inaccessible the formal Episcopal liturgy was presumed to be by one raised in the more formless milieu of the "free" church tradition. But knowing that Lane Thomas was a member of All Souls encouraged Lise to take the risk. More than that, she had noticed, earlier in the week, the announcement that on this particular Sunday morning the new Associate Rector, Sandra Albright, would be preaching. Her subject: "To Forgive as We Are Forgiven."

Lise had read stories in the local newspaper, several weeks earlier, about the singular nature of Sandra Albright's appointment. It was still relatively rare, the reporter wrote, for a mainline congregation to call to its ordained staff a person who was openly gay or lesbian, and the fact that the call had received overwhelming support from the congregation—nearly 80% of those voting—made it all the more remarkable. The event had been picked up, the local story said, by media across the country.

It had stirred local controversy in the "Letters to the Editor" column, with some expressing righteous outrage, and others suggesting that homophobia was nothing more than a kind of primitivist instinct that had no place in civilized society. Although the issue was essentially abstract for her, and although she knew that her parents—or at least her father—would be in the company of the outraged, she had sided with the latter view.

Lise was curious about Sandra Albright. And it was to satisfy that curiosity, rather than out of any serious spiritual motivation, that she entered the sanctuary of All Souls on this Sunday morning.

The service, strikingly different from the one to which she was accustomed in her father's church, was impressive, even moving in a way in which she had seldom been moved in church. Here there was a kind of dignity and formality that appealed to her. The clergy and the choir were vested; the service moved in an orderly way with set responses, prayers, and creed, as prescribed in the Book of Common Prayer; throughout the service there was an antiphonal relationship between clergy and congregation; and the organ and the choir provided moments of transcendence which lifted her spirit in ways it had seldom, if ever, been lifted on a Sunday morning. The passing of the Peace, where each member of the congregation turned to those who sat nearby and offered them "the peace of Christ," often with an embrace, was to this child of Baptist tradition the most remarkable, and in some ways the most moving, of all.

Responsibilities for leading the worship were shared between the Rector and Associate Rector, one offering the prayers, the other reading the Old and New Testament Lessons. Sandra Albright added to the impressiveness of the service. Her voice was firm and clear, her manner was reverent but not somber, and her obvious self-assurance set up in Lise an excited anticipation of what would follow.

"Imagine," she thought in some astonishment, "I'm actually looking forward to a sermon!"

She wasn't disappointed. Over the years her common experience in reflecting on the sermon, as she left the church Sunday after Sunday, had been to say to herself, "What had all that to do with me?" This time it was as if Sandra Albright had known Lise Warner would be in the congregation that morning, knew what life issues Lise was struggling with, knew what word Lise needed to hear.

It has been common, in her experience, for the sermon to fade from memory before she reached the door of the church. This time Sandra Albright's words burned in Lise's consciousness, both as judgment and as promise. She couldn't remember them all, of course, and she determined to return to the church later in the week to pick up a copy of the sermon, which had been promised for distribution. She wanted to read it—to experience it—again, and perhaps again.

What had Sandra Albright said about forgiveness that so touched Lise, both where she hurt and where she hoped?

This, among other things:

Relationships are fragile. Even in the very best of circumstances, things go wrong, sometimes thoughtlessly and inadvertently, at other times impulsively and deliberately. Love can only grow, can only be sustained in us and among us, where there is both the will to forgive, and the willingness to be forgiven.

It is important to be clear that forgiveness does not mean to forget or to overlook. To do either is to pretend that violations of intimacy aren't real, aren't serious. They are! And no loving relationship is possible for us where our offenses against intimacy go unacknowledged, as if they didn't matter. They do! Pretense and lies—whether told to oneself or to the other in a relationship—feed exploitation. Love is bound to truth.

Stripped of its sentimental accretions, forgiveness is essentially truthtelling and truth-hearing. It means, if I have been hurt by some action or inaction of the other, I must be willing to say, as soon as possible, and as directly and specifically as I can, what that hurt is. Depending on the nature of the hurt, that truth-telling may be accompanied by some anger. And I must make it clear, despite my hurt and anger, that I am prepared to keep all of the human options open between us. That's what forgiveness is.

And this:

No relationship can survive in which hurts are held and nurtured by the offended one, where there is something in the relationship that has to be lived down. Similarly, no relationship can survive in which the offender refuses to hear and acknowledge the truth of his offenses. Love can grow only where forgiveness is both given and received, which means that rather than having something to live down, the offender has found someone to live with.

And this:

Offering forgiveness is tough to do. It's hard to give up the satisfaction that comes from a feeling of moral superiority in the presence of the offender; even hard to give up the momentary satisfaction of wounded pride. But such feeling is like the snake that swallows its own tail: there is some nourishment in it, but it is definitely subject to the law of diminishing returns.

And finally this:

Life is always a gift, whether in that act in which we are first created, or in those continuing acts of forgiveness by means of which our lives must continually be restored and renewed. Forgiveness is the cement that holds life together, since it is the refusal to accept any relationship as permanently broken. In spite of the risk, the vulnerability, the moral nakedness forgiveness requires, our lives are in ultimate danger only if we refuse to offer each other the gift of life, only if we refuse to receive that gift from each other.

And when forgiveness is both offered and received, it can, indeed, work miracles.

Following the benediction and recessional, almost no one rose to leave the sanctuary. The congregation sat quietly while the organist played Karg-Elert's "Now Thank We All Our God" as the postlude to the service. Lise Warner thought that was quite remarkable. She had never before heard an organ postlude she thought was worth sitting still for. But then, she had never heard an organist who seemed to have such mastery of her instrument as this one. She felt strangely moved by the magnificent cadences of the music, which ended with a thundering affirmation, the 32-foot bass pedals giving the music a physical impact to match its aural presence.

Enthusiastic applause greeted the organist as the postlude ended, and she nodded modestly to the congregation in response. Then people felt free to greet their neighbors in the pews and to move about the sanctuary.

An informal coffee hour followed the 11 o'clock service at All Souls, and now Lise Warner let herself be carried along in the stream of people who, she thought, were probably heading for Cranmer Hall where the coffee tables were set up.

She had hoped for at least a word with Sandra Albright. Since the ministers were not shaking hands with departing congregants at the sanctuary door, Lise assumed that that was where Sandra might be found.

She was right. There was quite a line of people waiting to speak to the morning's preacher, and Lise decided to wait until there were fewer people around. What she wanted to say to Sandra Albright was, well, a bit personal, and she preferred not to say it in the hearing of others.

Although she wasn't a devoted coffee drinker, she thought she would feel more comfortable, standing about in the Hall waiting for an opportune moment, if she had something in her hands.

There were several coffee lines, and she was delighted to recognize the back of Professor Lane Thomas at the end of one of them. She went and stood behind him. He was next in line, so she waited to speak to him until he was served.

Once he had his coffee in hand and was about to step away from the table, Lise said, "Professor Thomas?" Lane turned abruptly, and found Lise Warner standing mere inches away, closer to her than he had ever stood before. Flustered, he spilled his coffee.

Fortunately his saucer contained the spill. "I'm terribly sorry,"

Lise said, "I didn't mean to startle you." She felt surprise and embarrassment at Lane's apparent discomfiture. But he said at once, "No, no. It's not your fault at all. And in fact, I'm delighted to see you. I've been thinking about you—well, that is, about our conversation in the Campus Union earlier in the week. How are things going for you?"

He led her away from the serving lines into a quieter corner of the room, as she replied, "Better, I think. I'm getting some of the things we talked about resolved, at least in my mind. And the sermon this morning—that was a real help."

"She's impressive, isn't she," said Lane referring to Sandra Albright. "And she's just as impressive out of the pulpit as in it.

"By the way," he went on, "you and she have something in common. She majored in Comparative Literature as an undergraduate at Macalester College. Then later, at the University of Chicago Divinity School where she went for her pastoral training, she found out about their doctoral program in Religion and the Arts and stayed on to take a Ph.D., specializing in religion and literature. In fact, you'll be glad to know that I've invited her to be a guest lecturer in our class later in the term."

"Gosh, now I really am impressed," said Lise. "How do you know so much about her?"

"I was on the Search Committee that recommended her call to the parish," said Lane. "She was far and away the strongest candidate we looked at. The fact that she's a lesbian has been getting most of the attention, of course, and I regret that only because it may obscure her very considerable professional qualifications. Maybe after the novelty of the lesbian issue wears off, people will begin to see what a multidimensional talent she is.

"Would you like to meet her?" Lane asked. "The group around her seems to have thinned quite a bit. Let's go over."

Lise couldn't have been more pleased—not just to be meeting Sandra Albright, but to be introduced by Professor Thomas. Pretty special, she thought.

"Sandra, here's someone I'd like you to know," Lane said, as they found her momentarily alone. "This is Lise Warner. She's a senior at Macauley. She's an excellent student and, like you, she's interested in Comparative Literature. Lise, this is Dr. Albright."

"Lise, this is Sandra," said the older woman with a smile, gently mocking Lane with her tone while offering her hand to Lise. And then she said to Lane, "I know all about academic formalities, but we don't stand on titles here. Not even that 'Reverend' stuff, if I have my way about it. It has always seemed so, well, pretentious."

And then to Lise: "I'm really very glad to meet you and to find somebody else who understands the agonies and ecstasies of CompLit. We'll have to meet soon to talk about our favorite authors."

Lise was immediately warmed by Sandra's greeting. She was excited to discover that the woman who was such an impressive professional in the pulpit was also a very accessible human being out of the pulpit.

"I'd like that very much," said Lise. "And I want you to know how helpful I found what you had to say about forgiveness. It sounded as if you surely must have know I would be here this morning and had prepared your words especially for me."

"Well," said Sandra, "that gives us something else to talk about when we get together. How about settling on a date right now? Monday is my day off. If you're free at noon tomorrow, I'll make lunch for us at my apartment."

Lise eagerly agreed. At this point, a few more parishioners appeared to greet the preacher of the morning. Lise and Lane said their good-byes to Sandra and moved toward the door of Cranmer Hall.

"What did I tell you," said Lane. "She is impressive, isn't she." Lise felt affirmed by their meeting—affirmed by Lane as well as by Sandra, and she thanked Lane warmly. He was aware that he liked being with her very much and was reluctant to leave. But Anne Armstrong was expecting him for Sunday brunch, so he excused himself and went on his way. They parted, with Lise saying, "I'll see you in class tomorrow." Lane, remembering Lise's classroom attentiveness, thought to himself, "You always do!"

This had been quite a morning, Lise reflected. She had been personally affirmed by the experience: by Sandra Albright's sermon and by the inviting way Sandra had received her; by Lane Thomas's warm friendliness and by his description of her as "an excellent student."

Lise couldn't remember another Sunday morning when she had felt this good on leaving church.

MONDAY

CHAPTER EIGHT
AN UNEXPECTED QUESTION

Sandra Albright's apartment was scarcely a ten-minute walk from the Macauley College campus. At 11:40 on Monday morning, Lise Warner left her campus dormitory, deliberately giving herself time to enjoy the sunshine of a late-fall Midwest day. Most of the color was gone from the maples and sweet gum trees, but the day had begun unseasonably warm and she was glad for the break from the sequence of three morning classes with which she always began her week.

One of them was Lane Thomas's "Theological Issues in Contemporary Literature." As usual, she had found Lane's lecture interesting as well as provocative. Although she had read more widely in contemporary literature than most fourth-year undergraduates, partly out of her own interest and partly the result of her CompLit major, before this class it had never occurred to her to think about those literary works theologically.

The discussion on this particular morning had been on themes from Albert Camus' *The Fall* and H. Richard Niebuhr's *The Meaning of Revelation*. As she walked toward the Albright apartment, she thought how remarkable it was, as Lane had suggested in his lecture, that the Frenchman, atheist as he was, had nevertheless attributed to Jean-Baptiste Clamence, his central—indeed, his only—character in *The Fall*, the very experiences Niebuhr had described as the classic marks of divine revelation. It was almost as if, in spite of himself, the novelist had intuited something more in the mystery of things than his own philosophy permitted.

She would have to look at the two together, test whether or not she could buy Lane's reported discovery of coincidence in them. She was disposed to accept his suggestion in advance, since Lane had proved to be a fair-minded interpreter both of literature and of theology. But Lise liked to make decisions for herself. She knew, from her own reading of two of Camus' other novels, *The Stranger* and *The Plague*, how often the Frenchman used biblical allusions, and never more so than in *The Fall*. She knew that as a young man he had written a thesis on Christian Neoplatonism. Obviously the Frenchman knew the biblical tradition well. Its imagery had entered importantly into his literary imagination. She would have to see for herself whether or not, in spite of himself, this notion of an intuition within and beyond the mystery really made sense.

Whether, finally, it made sense or not, it was an intriguing idea, and at the very least it offered a fresh perspective from which to make a careful examination of both the novel and the theological treatise. That fresh perspective was the main intellectual value Lise was finding in Lane's course.

Lise arrived at Sandra Albright's door a few minutes before noon and, recalling Sandra's warm reception of her in the church parlor the previous morning, she thought it would be acceptable to be just a bit early. She rang the bell, identified herself through the intercom, and a buzzer admitted her into the apartment hallway. Sandra was waiting for her at the open door of the apartment, and the warmth and informality that Lise had experienced the day before was very much in evidence. Sandra's 5'8" frame was slimmed by sweater and jeans, and with her hair in a long braid along the right side of her face, she looked younger than her 34 years.

"Lise, how nice to see you again. Come in. Let me take your jacket. Our meal is in the oven," Sandra said in welcoming.

"I'm really glad to be here," Lise replied. "It was very generous of you to invite me for lunch. When we met yesterday I was only hoping for a few minutes to talk with you about your sermon. But this is a real bonus!"

"I'm sure there's lots for us to talk about—probably more than we can manage in a single conversation," said Sandra. "But we can keep the talk going beyond today.

"I'm intrigued that you're majoring in Comparative Literature.

In fact, I'm envious that you are in a program that gives you time to read and think. I haven't had that luxury since I finished my degree in Chicago. My life is so busy with doing that it doesn't leave as much space as I would like for reading and thinking.

"Come into the kitchen," Sandra said, leading the way. "The quiche should be ready. We can sit right down and dig into the conversation as well as the food." After she had served the hot dish, Sandra offered a brief prayer of thanks, and they began the meal.

Knowing that Lane Thomas and Sandra Albright were friends, and sensing that the issues she had been reflecting on from Lane's morning lecture would match Sandra's comparative interests, Lise summarized briefly Lane's hypothesis about Albert Camus and Richard Niebuhr.

Sandra was an attentive listener and a sensitive responder. "That's a very helpful juxtaposition, making a connection between those two important and apparently diverse thinkers," said Sandra. "It certainly stretches my imagination to think what they would have had to say to each other, had they ever met. How absolutely marvelous it would have been to eavesdrop on their conversation.

"There's one danger that has to be avoided in all of this," Sandra went on, "and knowing Lane, I'm sure he has taken full account of it. I've known some people—preachers mainly, I regret to say— who have wanted to make critics of Christianity out to be crypto-Christians. That's not fair. In fact, I think it's intellectually dishonest. If someone like Camus says, 'I'm no Christian; in fact, I'm an atheist,' we have to take that very seriously rather than presuming that we know his mind better than he knows it himself.

"It's still possible that Lane's discovery of a coincidence between Camus and Niebuhr is valid, but that doesn't make a secret believer out of Camus. The issue isn't so much what the coincidence might mean either to Camus or to Niebuhr, but what it means to you, to me, as readers and as persons who are trying to be thoughtful about this living mystery into which we have all been cast."

"You're right about Dr. Thomas," said Lise. "He warned us of that danger at the beginning of the course, and he has repeated the warning regularly throughout the term. And I know about the danger at first hand. I have heard my father fall into that temptation when talking about Gandhi in his sermons. On more than one occasion he has said that Gandhi was a Christian without knowing it. Even at the time—before I came to college—I couldn't imagine how one could be a Christian without knowing it, since I had assumed that one becomes a Christian only by making a conscious commitment."

"So, your father is a minister?" Sandra asked.

"A conservative Baptist," Lise replied. "In fact, a very conservative Baptist. And that has become an increasing problem for me, especially since I have come to Macauley. I don't know what to do with it, and that's one of the things I wanted to talk with you about.

"Yesterday your sermon on forgiveness really hit me where I hurt. I'm pretty angry with my father, though I've never been able to express that anger to him directly. He'd be shocked, hurt, if he knew how I sometimes feel.

"It's not his conservatism as such that bothers me. It's what seems to be the mindlessness of it all. It's as if some years ago he adopted this theological posture, found that it got him where he wanted to go, and never thought about it again. My mother has adopted it, too, with even less thought, because she has been expected—he has expected her—to be the kind of wife he thought he needed for his own advancement to larger and larger churches. And she has given in to that kind of role-playing—started playing it so many years ago that she probably can't remember a time when she was ever any different.

"And it has worked for him. He now has a parish with 1,500 members, the largest Baptist church in the entire Midwest region. He was recently elected Chairman of the Board of Trustees of Macauley College, undoubtedly because of his influence in the denomination, and because he represents the kind of new conservative image the College wants to project."

Lise paused for a moment, but Sandra was listening intently and had no inclination to interrupt what was obviously a deeply felt recital of long-held grievances. Lise went on.

"I resent what my father has done to himself, the person thoughtless ambition has driven him to be. I resent what he has done to my mother, and I resent her willingness to copy the image he has drawn for her. And I resent his attempt to make me in that image, too.

"Well, I simply won't be that kind of person," Lise said, emphasizing each word as if it were a covenant with herself. "I'm not in rebellion against the Christian faith. It makes sense to me that 'we are made by Love for love.' That's the way one of the readings for Professor Thomas's class summarized the Gospel message. But I have come to believe that doubt is an essential part of faith, and without doubt there can be no genuine believing.

"My father simply wouldn't understand that. He hasn't permitted himself an iota of doubt for twenty years, and the result in him isn't faith at all but lifeless theological formulas."

Now Lise stopped, her energy temporarily spent from this outpouring of emotion. She put her head down, and there were tears on her cheeks.

Sandra Albright let Lise have the moment. When she sensed that the younger woman had gathered herself, Sandra said, "It would be presumptuous of me to say that I know how you feel, because your feelings are very much your own. But I can imagine your pain, the combination of love and anger that you must be feeling toward both your father and your mother. I can imagine your grief at what you sense has been lost—the realness that may have gone out of their lives, the threatened loss of realness in your own life, the loss to you of both parents as resources for empathy and understanding.

"I can imagine it," Sandra said, "because it has happened to me, too. And while this is your moment and not mine, at least I want you to know that I have been through—in some ways am still going through—this same kind of grieving. For me the issue isn't theological, because my parents have no active religious faith. It has to do with my lesbianism, with their disappointed hopes for me, their desire that I should pretend to be something I am not, and the alienation that occurred when I refused to pretend to live life on their terms and insisted on living it on my own."

"What did you do?" Lise asked, drying her tears with the tissue Sandra offered.

"I cried a lot," said Sandra. "I suspect you've done that, too. I pounded pillows to release my anger, since I had never learned to express anger directly to my parents. And then at some point I realized that, however different they and I might be, they were still my parents, and I wanted to find some way to be myself with them, if they were willing.

"That meant that I had to forgive them for the hurt I experienced in their rejection of me. And it meant that I had to forgive myself for the guilt I felt at having disappointed them. Eventually it resulted in the sermon I preached yesterday morning."

"And did it work?" Lise wanted to know. "I mean, were they able to respect you, to accept you, in your difference from them? Were you able to respect and accept them in spite of their disapproval?"

"Not at first," Sandra said, sadness in her voice. "In fact, not for quite a long time. It wasn't any easier for me to give up my resentment of them than it was for them to give up their disappointment in me. Both they and I had an emotional investment in our own positions, and we were reluctant to give them up. Pride can be a formidable enemy of love, you know.

"But gradually I came to the view I expressed in my sermon yesterday. Relationships are fragile, and no more so than between parents and child. If I wanted to have parents, and if I was willing to be a daughter, there had to be truth-telling and truth-hearing on both sides. I had to be willing to tell them, as I had never learned, never dared to do before, just how things were with me. I had to let them know not only how deeply I care about them and how much

I want their love, but also how deep my anger with them has been, how rejected I have felt.

"And at the same time, I had to be willing to hear from them the depth of their own disappointment, their own anger with me, and their own caring.

"It was pretty tough, pretty intense for a while, and we couldn't stand to be in each other's presence for more than an hour. But because they and I had decided, quite independently, that we were willing to practice the difficult skills of truth-telling and truth-hearing until they got easier, they did get easier. And now we can stand to be together, even enjoy being together, for a full day at a time. That's real progress!

"Having told and having heard, by some grace we had to be willing to give up our investment in the old hurts, to be willing to start all over again. I have had to find a way to say, 'These are my parents, God bless them!' They have had to find a way to say, 'This is our lesbian daughter, God bless her!'"

Both women were silent for a long moment. Then Lise looked intently into the older woman's eyes and said, "Sandra, how does a woman know she's a lesbian?"

After a hesitation, Sandra said quietly, "Is that a question about me—or is it a question about you?"

Lise didn't answer at once. She was startled by her own boldness. It was not a question she had consciously come to ask. Yet there it was, arising suddenly out of some unexplored depth. She could only say, "I—I don't know. Both, I suppose. It's not a question I have ever asked myself before, let alone asked anyone else. And having asked it, I've embarrassed myself and I'm sure I've embarrassed you. I'm sorry, very sorry." And Lise began to cry.

"No, Lise," Sandra said at once, "you haven't embarrassed me at all, and as far as I'm concerned, there is no need for you to feel embarrassed either. That's one of the problems with our good, middle-class, Protestant culture. We have persuaded people—especially young people—that the question you've asked is improper, even perverse. So it's no wonder that there is a lot of confusion, of anguish, of despair about sexual identity when the issue can't be explored freely, when young women and men can't come to their own independent conclusions about who they are."

By the time Sandra had stopped talking, Lise had composed herself. "Thanks," she said, wiping her eyes. "I appreciate your openness and understanding. I don't know of anyone else I could have put my question to."

Sandra said, "There is something I have to make clear, if you and I are to continue our conversation now or in the future, as I would like to do. You know that I have publicly acknowledged my own lesbianism. It was an issue in my call to serve All Souls Church. The way they have accepted me, and their decision even before I came to be an opening and affirming congregation, welcoming into membership all persons whether straight or gay, frees me to deal openly with the issue in my ministry here.

"But I have no interest in leading you to any particular conclusion about your own sexuality. In fact, my sexual orientation is irrelevant to our discussion. It wouldn't matter if I were gay or straight. All I can do, all I'm willing to do, is to help you clarify the questions, so that you can arrive at answers that are really, authentically your own, just as I did.

"I just want to be sure you understand that, before we go any farther."

"Thanks," said Lise. "I do understand, and I'm grateful for your willingness to let me be who I am. It's the problem of being who someone else wants me to be that I'm trying to escape. So I really welcome your openness, your objectivity."

"Good," said Sandra. "Then we can continue our conversation. And I'd like to propose that we continue this particular topic in my study at the church, just to make it clear that we are dealing with the question you asked on a professional basis.

"That doesn't at all mean that I don't want to be your friend, or be in touch with you informally. I do, and I suspect we'll find lots of interests in common. So let's just keep this relationship going on two tracks, as it were. How does that seem to you?"

Lise agreed enthusiastically. They set a time, two days later, for Lise to meet with Sandra in her office, and they then turned to conversation about their respective literary interests. The conversation was so lively and engrossing, in fact, that it was three o'clock before either of them knew it. They said their good-byes with genuine reluctance, agreeing to meet again in two days.

Lise walked thoughtfully back to her dormitory. It had been a remarkable afternoon, she thought. Where had her question about lesbianism come from? She didn't know. But she certainly intended to find out.

CHAPTER NINE

CONSPIRATORS

A short distance from Sandra Albright's apartment, a different kind of noontime conversation was going on. Three members of the Macauley College faculty had met by prearrangement at the Towne Grill. Just two blocks from the Macauley campus, the Grill was a popular luncheon spot for faculty members who wanted more privacy—a haven from student interruptions, less surveillance by fellow teachers on who was talking to whom, less speculation on what they might be talking about—than the Campus Union offered. The Grill had an efficient kitchen that served up moderately tasty meals in reasonably short order, and the high sides of each booth made it unlikely that a conversation in one would be overheard by diners in adjacent booths.

As it happened, these conditions were of special importance on this Monday to Lane Thomas, Anne Armstrong, and Jim Denison, who had agreed to meet and talk further about the policy announcement made by President Kean at Friday's Faculty Meeting.

After orders of soup and salad all around, Jim Denison plunged at once into the subject of the moment. His irritation over the presidential announcement had increased as the intervening weekend progressed, and now on Monday Denison couldn't decide which was the more appalling, the know-nothing substance of the new policy, or the arrogance of its unilateral promulgation by President and Trustees.

"I've been a member of the Macauley faculty for 17 years," said Jim, "and I've seen some pretty stupid, opportunistic things done by administrations over the years, but this is undoubtedly the dumbest, most unprincipled move that has yet been made in all that time. And the crashing irony of it is that it is being made by an administration that talks loudest about its Christian character. It's enough to make me an atheist."

"Yes, but how do you really feel about it, Jim?" said Anne, trying to strike a somewhat lighter note, thinking that they might get farther with their conversation if the level of its emotional intensity were lowered a bit.

And then she added, "I think we have to be as critical of faculties as we are of administrations. Why do you suppose administrators regularly get away with this kind of thing? Because a college faculty is about the most politically naive crowd you can find anywhere. We talk a hard line, but when it comes to organizing for confrontation, the troops just aren't there. We are really a bunch of individual entrepreneurs. All of our talk about 'academic freedom' is really just so much professional solipsism, an insistence on being left alone to do things our own individual ways. For most faculty members, 'academic freedom' means, 'Nobody—no administrator, no teaching colleague—can tell me how to do things in my classroom.' So given this fundamental faculty bias in favor of professional aloneness, this refusal to sublimate personal convenience to a larger, more inclusive good, when the time for confrontation comes of course the troops aren't there, and administrators can work their institutional wills with virtual impunity.

"Do you wonder," Anne added with a wry smile, "why some administrators are 'academic freedom's' best friend?"

"I wish you were wrong," said Jim Denison, now calmed by Anne's sober analysis, "because your argument certainly doesn't do much for my self-regard as an academic professional. Unfortunately, honest reflection on these 17 years of 'professing' tells me you're right."

"So," Lane Thomas interceded, "if Kean and the Trustees have taken their unilateral action on the assumption that the reaction of the faculty will be as uncoordinated and as harmless as usual, how do we get their attention? Come to that, given your analysis, how do we even get the faculty's attention?"

"Oddly enough," said Anne, "the Trustees may be easier than the faculty. Over the weekend I talked with a couple of my colleagues in political science, and with one of our departmental alums from several years ago who is now an attorney in town. Our best strategic estimate is that we should take a two-pronged approach: seek an injunction against the Trustees in Superior Court on the ground of breach of contract, and ask the U.S. District Court to issue an injunction against the policy on the ground that it would violate students' civil rights."

In their telephone conversation on Saturday morning, Anne had already sketched for Lane the outline of the "breach of contract" approach, and she summarized it now for Jim Denison. It came down to this: responsibility for determining the learning arrangements within the college has been given by the Trustees to the faculty; one of the historic distinctives of Macauley, as of other liberal arts colleges, is that its intended learnings encompass the personal growth of students, as well as their intellectual growth. Therefore, decisions about policy touching personal growth are as much the province of the faculty as are decisions about intellectual growth.

"So," Anne concluded, "whatever one might think about the issue of homosexuality itself, for the Trustees to make a unilateral decision about it is to breach its contract with the faculty."

Jim Denison whistled softly. "I like the sound of that. It would hit them where they are likely to hurt. But it would be a pretty ambitious undertaking. Do you and your advisers think we could win two suits like that?"

"We don't have any idea whether or not we could win if the two actions actually came to trial," said Anne. "For example, in the Federal case, the Board would probably argue that, given the college's historic Baptist connection, it is permitted by the religious freedom clause of the Constitution to discriminate on the basis of sexual orientation because, in their view, the Bible declares homosexuality to be a sin and Christians are required to separate themselves from deliberate sinners."

"How about proposing to the Trustees that they should stone

Charles Kean!" said Lane in exasperation. "If I remember correctly, Mrs. Kean had been married before. The New Testament says that whoever marries a divorced woman commits adultery, and in the Old Testament the punishment for adultery is stoning. Selective biblicism makes me sick!"

"It's possible," Anne went on, her smile acknowledging Lane's point, "that the mere threat of legal action would have a powerful effect on the President and the Trustees. It would make a public issue both of homosexuality and of their own corporate misfeasance. The last thing the Trustees will want, at a time when they are trying to create a positive image to attract students and money to this place, is for that image to be put at risk by the prospect of an extended dispute in public. Parents and donors are likely to be pretty reluctant to support a college where there is a disruptive squabble between faculty and administration."

"So, where do we get the plaintiffs for these two actions?" Lane Thomas wanted to know.

Anne didn't reply while a server set the soups and salads on the table in front of them. When the server had left, Anne said, "Ideally the breach-of-contract suit should be supported by a majority of the members of the faculty. But that's not likely to happen. It's not only the professional isolationism, the lack of a sense of common purpose, that I spoke of earlier. It's also a fear many will have that they will face arbitrary administrative reprisal, in one form or another, if they oppose Charles Kean and the Board openly.

"It would be best," Anne added, "if we could identify one person—preferably a very senior person, somebody with real standing in the College, who would give the action a credible public face—to file a class-action suit on behalf of the faculty. Then we would need to recruit individual faculty members to stand behind it and constitute the 'class' on whose behalf the action is to be taken. We wouldn't need the entire faculty to make the threat real, but we would need a substantial number—fifteen at least."

"We can't expect untenured people to sign up," said Jim

Denison, nodding in Lane's direction. "Some of the rest of us are less vulnerable. I'm ready and willing. I assume you are too." He looked at Anne.

"Of course!" she said.

"Wait a damned minute," said Lane, who had become increasingly enthused as Anne had described the proposed tactics. "Don't write me off so quickly. I appreciate your concern for my rather fragile status, but I care about this too, you know. Anyway, I'm already in the 'doubtful' category when it comes to tenure, partly because I don't fit the current theological mold in this place, and partly because I shared in the recommendation to call Sandra Albright to the ministry of the All Souls Church. So I probably don't have much to lose from one more apparent indiscretion. Count me in!"

"There is a possible complication in the request for a federal injunction on civil rights grounds," Anne explained. "We might have to find a student willing to be the plaintiff in filing a class-action suit, since only a student would have standing with the court to file the request on behalf of other students. In other words, it would have to be filed by someone who would actually suffer discrimination if the policy were not enjoined."

"Then it would need to be an avowed homosexual," said Jim Denison. "That might be hard to come by. But I suppose we can take one step at a time—solve that one when and if we come to it."

"This whole thing sounds pretty expensive. How do we pay for the legal costs?" Lane Thomas wanted to know.

Anne said, "The local attorney we talked with is so intrigued by this whole thing—and, not just incidentally, is so irritated with Charles Kean's effort to turn the College into a bastion of fashionable conservatism—that he's prepared to take it on *pro bono.*"

"So how do we proceed from this point?" Jim Denison asked.

Anne had thought about that question ahead of time. "I suggest that each of us make up a list of the tenured faculty we think might be willing to risk the kind of confrontation with President and Trustees we're talking about by supporting the legal actions," she proposed. "Then we can meet again in a day or two to compare lists. If a name appears on at least two of our lists, one of us should agree to have a confidential talk with that person, see what kind of initial reaction we get. And," she added, "the best person to file the class action should be among those names."

"In the meantime," said Lane, "shouldn't we keep this strictly among ourselves?"

"Absolutely," said Anne. "If any hint of possible legal action gets out, we'll lose the force and effect of a preemptive strike. As I said earlier, I'm not confident we could actually win either action, but the mere threat of them may give us the negotiating leverage with the Trustees we need to turn back their mindlessness."

Agreeing to meet again at the same place and time in two days, they turned their attention to the food in front of them, which they attacked with surprising vigor. An awareness of their shared commitment, and a sense that they might not be powerless after all, seemed to have added a fresh edge to their appetites.

*

When Religion Department chairman Ralph Dwight had ended his interview with Lane Thomas on the previous Friday afternoon, he sat at his desk for a time, rehearsing what Lane had said about his role in that recent unfortunate—no, inexcusable!—business at All Souls Church. While Dwight had clearly questioned Lane's biblical apologetic for homosexuality, he congratulated himself that, for the most part, he had restrained his irritation. Time enough for that later. But this young man will not do, he mused. He simply will not do!

But how, in view of Lane's tenure candidacy, to handle what would be a very delicate situation, was the question. He picked up the telephone and dialed a line that went directly into the office of President Charles Kean, bypassing Kean's secretary. Dwight was the only person within the College, except for its business and development vice-presidents, who even knew such a number existed. Not even Academic Dean Morton Emmons, a holdover from pre-

Kean days considered by the President to be ideologically unreliable, was aware of it.

After standard pleasantries, Ralph Dwight said, "Charles, I've just had an hour's talk with Lane Thomas. He brought me his tenure dossier, and this was the department chairman's required debriefing prior to transmitting the dossier to the Committee on Promotion and Tenure. I still haven't written my recommendation which must accompany the dossier, and I don't want to do that until you and I have a chance to talk. I probably can't hold off sending the dossier to the Committee much beyond the first of the week, so I'm calling to see if you might have some free time for me on Monday. Frankly, I think Thomas is trouble, serious trouble, especially in view of the trustee policy action you will be announcing at the faculty meeting this afternoon." Dwight was the only person within the College to whom the President had confided the pending announcement.

"I'll certainly see you if I can. Just let me check my calendar," said Kean. After a moment he came back on the line. "How about lunch in my office on Monday at one o'clock? I'll send over to the Union for sandwiches."

So it had been arranged. And now, on Monday afternoon, Kean and Dwight were settled at the conference table in the President's office, sandwiches and coffee before them.

"What's your urgent concern about Lane Thomas?" the President invited, not wanting to waste time in a busy afternoon. "He seems like an inoffensive young man."

"Not as inoffensive as he may have seemed up to now," Ralph Dwight replied. "I doubt that you knew at the time how deeply Lane Thomas was involved in that deplorable business at All Souls Church some weeks ago, calling a lesbian to its ministry. Bad enough to permit a woman to be ordained in the first place, worse by far when she has admitted to a perverse lifestyle."

"Disgraceful business!" the President ejaculated. "Unscriptural—anti-scriptural, really. But then, what should one expect of Episcopalians! With the church so near the campus, I felt contaminated by it. One of the reasons I urged the homosexuality policy on the Trustees was that I thought we had an obligation to set a higher standard, try to counteract the influence of that cesspool of heterodoxy just three blocks from here. Are you telling me Lane Thomas was somehow involved in that business?"

"Right at the heart of it, in fact. He was a member of the search committee that recommended calling Sandra Albright. And not just a passive member either, to judge by what he said to me when we talked in my office last Friday afternoon. While he apparently hadn't given the issue much thought before the search began months ago, it's clear that he had become an active apologist for calling the lesbian by the time the process was completed.

"In fact," said Dwight, exasperation edging his voice, "he even had the effrontery to tell me that, at best, the Bible is indecisive in its view of homosexuality. It was an astonishingly brash performance, and it was only with great difficulty that I restrained myself from telling him so!"

"And you think this passion of the recent convert may lead Thomas to mount some kind of active protest against the new trustee policy?" the President wanted to know. "Could he create a serious problem? Does he have any real influence within the faculty? Would the result be any more than a blip on our screen? How many divisions does Professor Thomas have?" Kean's penchant for metaphor was in active evidence.

"It's hard to say what his own personal influence is," Dwight replied, "but he has some influential friends. You probably know that he and Anne Armstrong are an occasional item in the faculty social scene, and she's much respected by her colleagues in the Social Science Division. And Lane has an active friendship with Jim Denison, who is attractive to some in the Humanities Division precisely because he's a maverick.

"But it's not just the immediate nuisance Lane Thomas could create," Dwight went on. "We could probably finesse that. I'm thinking about the longer-term result of having on the faculty someone who is not only unsympathetic but perhaps even actively hostile to the Christian mission you and the Trustees are shaping for Macauley—and in the Religion Department at that! Why should we institutionalize even a small grain of irritation"—Dwight was not above the occasional use of mixed-metaphor, perhaps in the hope of winning presidential approval by an imitative style—"by rewarding it with tenure?

"Under the circumstances, I couldn't agree with you more," Kean said. "I like the way you think. I wish you were the Academic Dean. Perhaps in a year or so...." The caesura was deliberate, and its implication was not lost on Ralph Dwight. He flushed with pleasure.

"The problem," said Dwight, "is how to keep tenure from happening. You and I both know that faculty committees regularly make favorable recommendations on tenure on the basis of the simple inoffensiveness of the candidate. It isn't necessary to be able to say anything really positive about him, so long as there isn't anything offensive to be said. Given that kind of standard, Lane Thomas is a shoo-in. His record isn't outstanding by my standards, but it's well above average by ordinary academic measures. And he hasn't circulated much socially while he's been here, so that most of the senior faculty acting on the recommendation won't know him well enough to have anything against him."

"So," said the President, "you are to write a cover letter to accompany his dossier. Then the faculty Committee on Promotion and Tenure reviews the dossier and sends its recommendation to me, and I take it to the Board for final action. Right?"

"Right," said Dwight, "which means that there are two problems. First, what can I say that neither supports nor rejects his candidacy? And then, what issue can you and the Board use so that, when tenure is refused, it avoids the appearance of an arbitrary reprisal?"

"What's Thomas's academic specialty?" the President wanted to know.

"It's what he calls 'theological aesthetics,'" Dwight replied.

"Good heavens," said Kean, "does anybody know what that means?"

"He works at the interface between religion and the arts," Dwight explained.

"I didn't know religion and the arts had an interface," said Kean, who had been a corporate executive before appointment to Macauley's presidency. "All right, here's the drill," he went on, coming to a sudden decision. "With a slight hint from me, the Academic Affairs Committee of the Board will decide that we need, in the Department of Religion, a specialist in Evangelical Studies, to provide essential theological undergirding for the renewed mission of the College, and to assure constituency support. Even though young Thomas calls himself an evangelical, it's obvious from that shameful business at All Souls that he's theologically unreliable. Besides, evangelicalism isn't his specialty. And since fiscal constraints prevent us from adding another position in your department, we must—regrettably, of course—deny tenure to Professor Thomas in order to permit a new appointment which is essential to the integrity and future strength of Macauley. John Warner will be here on Friday for the announcement of the new policy on homosexuality, and I'll have a word with him about it then. What do you think?"

"That should do it," said Ralph Dwight with a broad smile.

"So here's my suggestion," the President went on. "The thing for you to do is to 'commend' Lane Thomas's dossier 'for the careful and prayerful consideration of the Committee on Promotion and Tenure.' If anybody reads that carefully, all you're saying is that they ought to take a hard look at it. That's probably the least you can say, and under the circumstances it's the most you can say. Then let the process work itself out from there on. If the Committee recommends tenure, as it probably will, it will be up to me to handle the matter with the Trustees."

"And you need be in no doubt about how that will turn out!"

WEDNESDAY

CHAPTER TEN
A NEW ALLY

Morton Emmons was Macauley College's Academic Dean.

Emmons' father had been a Presbyterian minister, and as an adolescent Morton had thought that he would follow his father into the ministry. But an undergraduate major in biology at The College of Wooster had fostered in him an agnostic habit. By the time he graduated, he had decided that he preferred to explore the mysteries of creation in a scientific laboratory rather than from a Presbyterian pulpit.

So it was to a doctoral program in biology at Ann Arbor, rather than to his father's old seminary at Princeton, that Morton went. He was appointed as an associate professor on Macauley's biology faculty twenty years ago, after a decade as an instructor in an undistinguished state college, and promoted to full professor a decade later. The Macauley appointment had come to him at a time when, despite the College's historic Baptist connection, its administration was disinclined to give much weight to that history. Emmons himself wasn't hostile to religion. He was merely skeptical, uncertain, unsure that the issue of cosmic meaning mattered much, so long as one was reasonably clear about important human and social meanings.

When Charles Kean was named Macauley's president, Morton Emmons had been the College's Academic Dean for just two years, and was due to retire in five more. Kean had decided not to upset an arrangement so recently made by appointing a Dean of his own choosing, and instead to take some time to consolidate his position in the College, looking forward to the opportunity, on Emmons' retirement, to have a Dean of more congenial outlook.

As it happened, just now Morton Emmons was a very troubled

Academic Dean. By temperament a noncontroversialist, he was also, by nature, a caring and compassionate man with a keenly honed sense of justice. So when President Kean had made his startling announcement at the conclusion of Friday's faculty meeting, Morton Emmons was torn. On the one hand, he considered the action of the Trustees to be arbitrary at best, deficient in essential humanity at worst, and his personal estimate was clearly on the latter side of that range. On the other hand, he shrank from the unpleasantness of confrontation.

As Academic Dean, putative leader of the faculty, he could hardly refuse to take notice of so gross a challenge to the humane and orderly traditions of a college like this one. But what should he do in measured response? That question was the single thought that had occupied Morton Emmons over the weekend and into the beginning of the week following the astonishing meeting.

By the time he went to bed at midnight on Tuesday, he had an answer. It was barely six-thirty a.m. on Wednesday morning when he picked up the telephone and dialed Jim Denison's number.

Despite their ideological differences—Emmons the devout agnostic, Denison the irreverent Catholic—they had frequently found common ethical ground over the years that had made them partners on many issues and led them not only to mutual respect but to deep friendship.

"Jim, it's Morton," the Dean said when a groggy Denison answered. "I know it's early, and I apologize for arousing you at this ungodly hour, but there's an urgent matter on which I'd like just a moment of your time."

"No need to apologize," said Denison, "although I had just gone ahead on points in a debate with the Pope. But I've put the dream on hold. I'm sure I can get back to it another night. At least I hope I can."

"My money's on you, as usual," said Emmons; and then he went on more seriously, "Ever since last Friday I've been obsessing about that mischievous business Charles Kean announced, trying to decide what I should—could—do about it. Well, I'm still not sure what I can do, but I'm absolutely certain about what I shall do, and I want to run it by you." Now Denison was totally awake.

Emmons said, "I intend to oppose the Trustee action openly. I want to find some effective way to say to the faculty, to the President and the Trustees, and to the public, that I consider this proposed new policy to be morally and educationally reprehensible, and that, in creating an invidious and suspicious atmosphere, it is likely to destroy whatever fragile sense of community we have been able to build here among teachers and learners. What they propose isn't liberal education. It's illiberal education of the worst kind!"

Emmons paused, and Jim Denison was silent on his end of the line for a brief moment. Then Denison said quietly, "Morton, you're a good man—a really good man. And a gutsy one, too."

"Oh, not really," said Emmons. "As strongly as I believe the things I just said, it won't be particularly risky for me to say them. I'm only a little over a year away from retirement. And if Kean wants to remove me from the Academic Dean's position, he's welcome to it and good luck to him with it, say I. Anyway, I'm still a tenured professor of biology.

"But even if it were risky," Emmons said, "I'd have to do it anyway. Charles Kean and John Warner can't be permitted to go without public challenge to their bigoted machinations. My only wish is that I were a religious man so that I could pronounce the appropriate theological anathemas on them.

"I know what I want to say," Emmons went on, "but I'm not sure when and where to say it, and that's one of the things I want to get your advice about."

"Morton, I'm grateful for your call. And you can't possibly know how providential—excuse the reference—it is. Three of us— Lane Thomas, Anne Armstrong, and I—with outreach to some of Anne's Political Science colleagues, have formed a small cabal for the purpose of frustrating the planned Friday public announcement. We've come up with a promising strategy." Jim summarized

Anne's proposal, and then said, "There's a role in those plans just made for you. We'll be meeting again at lunch today. Why don't you join us at the Towne Grill at 12:30. In the meantime, may I share your decision with them on a confidential basis?"

"Of course," said Emmons.

There was a new note of optimism in Jim Denison's voice as he concluded, "This is shaping up in a remarkably promising way. If you'll pardon my theological language, I think we may just possibly have Charlie Kean and the Board by the short hairs!"

CHAPTER ELEVEN

A TRAGIC TURN

In spite of other things on his mind, Lane Thomas couldn't shake the image of Lise Warner standing close in the coffee line in their chance encounter at church on Sunday morning. He was tempted to detain her after class on Monday but couldn't come up with a plausible reason. He thought about calling her at her dormitory room on Monday evening, and again on Tuesday, but couldn't figure out what he would say to her. In recent days, when Lane had tried to think about Lise, his mind seemed to go to mush. Ordinarily articulate, he bumbled even in imaginary conversations with her, making the prospect of a real conversation seem pretty formidable.

But it wasn't enough just to see her, lovely even at eight o'clock in the morning, sitting intently in the front row of his class, disconcerting him each time for the rest of the day. So he determined that on Wednesday he would tell her he wanted to follow up on their earlier conversation about Camus and to see how she was responding to more recent comparative themes in lectures and readings.

"Of course" she said, and he was pleased by the evident warmth of her response. She was free after her nine o'clock class and would be glad to meet him at 10 in the Campus Union.

Lane was there, in nervous anticipation, well before the appointed time. He had gone to his office after his eight o'clock class only long enough to drop off his lecture notes and was so absorbed in the anticipation of meeting Lise that he ignored a voice-mail message to call Jim Denison. "It can wait," Lane told himself. "Anyway, I'll be seeing him at noon at the Towne Grill."

So he went directly to the Campus Union and was on his second cup of coffee when Lise arrived, just as the Chapel bells were announcing the hour of ten. Lane got a diet soft drink for her and they settled into the booth he had chosen at the far end of the room.

"So," he said, "tell me what's been happening to you since we talked last. Did you get together with Sandra Albright?"

"Yes," said Lise, "lunch at her apartment on Monday was great. She's so easy to talk to. It was as comfortable as if we'd been old friends. I'm to meet her again tomorrow at her church office."

"And what about your father," Lane said, "any further contact with him?"

"I'm to see him on Friday," said Lise. "He's coming to make some kind of an announcement for the Trustees on Friday morning, and we're scheduled for lunch afterward. In fact, one of the reasons for seeing Sandra tomorrow is to prepare for that session with him, which is likely to be a difficult one for him as well as for me. I'm not willing to put off dealing with my feelings about him and Mother any longer, and I want to think through carefully just what I want to say to him and how I want to say it."

Lane sensed in Lise a strength and a determination that he hadn't detected the last time they talked, and he commented on it briefly. She seemed genuinely pleased. She knew she still had a long way to go, she said, but she was feeling surer about herself, and that was making a considerable difference in her outlook on everything—herself, her studies, her future after graduation.

Lane felt some obligation to talk about the work of his course, since that was the ostensible reason for inviting her to meet him, but somehow he couldn't bring himself to conjure up artificial issues. He thought she would be perceptive enough to sense their artificiality, and that would make it awkward for both of them. So he decided simply to let the conversation go wherever it would go, for as long as she seemed to be willing to continue it.

It was Lise who picked it up. "It doesn't seem fair," she said, "that teachers know a great deal about their students, but students know next to nothing about their teachers. Where did you go to college?"

Lane was somewhat startled by her energy and directness, but he was flattered and pleased by her unexpected interest in him. "When I was young, my parents and I lived in Seattle, and I went with them to an Episcopal church throughout those younger years. Although I was always interested in religion, I knew parish ministry wasn't my place. I'm sure that it was my early experience with the drama of the Anglican liturgy, as much as anything else, that stimulated my interest in religion and aesthetics and set me on what was to be the course of my professional life.

"I graduated from Lewis and Clark, a small, private, liberal arts college in Portland, Oregon, and a great place in every way. Fine teachers, and an impressive setting where one can look out across the campus to snow-capped Mt. Hood. I took a combined major in literature and religion and found people there who were willing to let me work at the intersections, rather than taking the customary narrow concentration on one or the other. I participated in the College's foreign study program—spent six months in Japan during my junior year. It made an enormous difference to me. Broadened my outlook, gave me habits of attention I'd never had before, because everything in Japan was new to me and had to be attended to if I was to survive in that unfamiliar place. For obvious reasons, it also sharpened my interest in comparative issues. You've been suffering some of the consequences of my comparative bent three times a week."

"Are you married? Do you have a family?" Lise wanted to know.

He was glad she asked. "No," he assured her quickly—perhaps a little too quickly, he realized; but then it was too late. "Never seemed to have time for the kind of relational intensity that results in marriage. I was too busy, first coping with demanding graduate studies in philosophy and theology at Claremont, and then trying to finish my dissertation in the first two years after I had actually begun teaching here. If you should decide to go on for a doctorate, let me urge you never to take on that double burden. It's just too much, and there is a constant danger that neither responsibility will be discharged as effectively as it deserves to be."

"What kind of a future do you see for yourself?" Lise asked, and Lane wished he could tell her that he had fantasies about her being a part of it. But instead he said, "Teaching is the only thing I've ever seriously wanted to do. That and the scholarship that goes with it. I'm interested in people, and I'm interested in ideas, and teaching is a critical point of interaction between the two. I consider myself enormously lucky to be a college teacher."

"Here at Macauley? I mean, do you see yourself teaching here for the long run?" Lise pressed.

Lane was aware that he was talking to the daughter of the Chairman of the Board of Trustees and that he should perhaps choose his words with special care. But he trusted Lise, for reasons he couldn't have articulated very well. And he believed that she trusted him, too.

Unfortunately! Her trust imposed some unwelcome limitations on him in their relationship, or at least he knew that it ought to: the obligation not to take advantage of her trust; not to exploit the respect, the admiration that was in her front-row intensity three times a week.

Would he honor it? Could he? Was that his decision alone? Shouldn't she have something to say about it? He didn't know. And her compelling presence at the table beside him only added to his unclarity.

So Lane said, "I really don't know. I'm up for tenure this year, and I'm not at all sure what the outcome of that will be. Frankly, I'm not even sure what I want the outcome to be. On the one hand, tenure is a sign of the professional esteem in which a teacher is held by an institution, and by colleagues within the institution. I want that; we all want it. At the same time, you must surely have realized, at least at some level in your consciousness, that my own religious outlook isn't exactly compatible with the recent turn toward the right in the official religious outlook of Macauley's new administration. Even though I identify myself with new evangelical impulses in the Episcopal tradition, I'm very uncomfortable with the effort at a conservative conformity that seems to be going on here. And I'm simply not prepared to become a conformist."

"I do know that," Lise said. "And it's a problem for me, too. Not so much because it's conservative. At the moment I don't know enough about theology to make precise distinctions between more conservative and less, between more liberal and less. I don't even know how to locate myself, except that I am not willing any longer to settle for the 'faith' that was fastened on me—my father's 'faith,' if it can be called that. It surely can't be called my mother's 'faith,' since she has been no more than a religious mime."

Lise went on. "I don't know whether or not what I have been learning in your class has a name—the faiths of Reinhold and Richard Niebuhr, of Dietrich Bonhoeffer and Paul Tillich and Frederick Buechner and the others—but if it has, I want it. I don't know whether or not what I heard last Sunday from Sandra Albright has a name, but it's where I want to be."

Lise looked intently at Lane. "I don't know whether or not, with your wider and longer experience, you can begin to understand my hunger for meanings that are believable, livable, but that's where I am. And I'm beginning to sense that possibly—just possibly—instead of my seeking them, meanings like that are reaching out to me, here and now."

In that instant, Lane Thomas knew he loved her.

He scarcely had time to savor that new realization when an enormous hubbub erupted among a group of students at the other end of the coffee shop. Voices were being raised, and Lane heard what he thought were cries of distress.

Lise said, "Excuse me. I'll just go and see what's happening."

Lane watched as she walked the length of the room to join the group, talked with one or two of the students, and then came unsteadily back to where he was waiting for her. She was ashen, and there was a look of confusion and incredulity on her face.

"It's about Rob Shaw," she said. "I can't believe it. They found him dead in his dorm room." She choked out the words. "He—he hanged himself."

Lane Thomas took a seriously shaken Lise Warner to his house and put in an urgent call to Sandra Albright, who promised to join them as soon as possible. She was there in twenty minutes, and Lane quickly and quietly filled her in on Rob Shaw: a senior like Lise, one of the most popular students on the campus, an accomplished goalie on Macauley's soccer team who had been responsible in a major way for Macauley's national soccer championship the year before.

When Lise had stopped crying and was feeling somewhat steadier, she was able to give Lane and Sandra a fuller account of what the students in the coffee shop had told her about Rob Shaw's death. She began quietly and slowly, occasionally touching her eyes with a tissue from the box Lane had provided.

"Yesterday," said Lise, "a student was told that on Friday of this week the Board of Trustees will announce a policy to expel from the College any student who is a homosexual, whether actively practicing or not."

Right! Lane thought bitterly. If you want a piece of information to get around, tell it to the faculty and tell them not to tell.

Lise went on. "In the note his roommate found, Rob said that he's known he was gay since early in his senior year in high school. A couple of people here from the same high school knew about it, too, though until now no one had ever said anything. Rob was waiting to 'come out' until he got admitted to law school, which was his great ambition. With fresh attention given to the issue as a result of the new policy, he was afraid his gayness might be talked about, he'd be expelled from Macauley, wouldn't get a degree, and his chance for law school destroyed. His family's disappointment in him would be crushing, for them as well as for him. He couldn't face that kind of shame and failure, he said, and taking his life was the lesser pain."

"This must be shocking to you," Sandra said. "Did you know Rob well?"

"Everybody knew him. He was one of the most popular men on the campus, and we were classmates, of course. But I didn't know him really well." Lise continued, obviously wanting to talk about him, perhaps to talk out some of her own pain. "Rob impressed me as a very gentle person, very polite, a really nice guy. He wasn't aggressive the way some campus athletes are. Maybe it was a reflection of his temperament that he played a defensive role on the soccer team. I just can't believe he's gone. He must have been terribly afraid, to take his own life. I can't even imagine that kind of desperation."

And then she turned to Lane. "Dr. Thomas, there's something I have to know. That rumor—the one that apparently led Rob to do what he did—about a new policy that would expel homosexual students. Is it true?"

It was the question Lane had been dreading, and he could see no way to avoid an honest answer. He hadn't been the one to break the confidentiality requested of the faculty by the President. It was out now—out in the most tragic way possible—and there was no point in denying it. So he simply said, "Yes."

"And this visit my father will be making on Friday. He told me he was coming to make some kind of an announcement to the College on behalf of the Trustees, and we're to meet for lunch afterward. Is that what he's coming for? To announce the new policy?" Lane had dreaded that question even more. And again he said simply, "Yes."

"Then he's responsible—he and the others on the Board—for adopting the policy?" It was a question, but it sounded to Lane like a conclusion already arrived at. Lane said, "I'm afraid the answer, again, is Yes. At least, that's what the faculty has been told. It's a question, in all fairness, that you should probably put to him."

"So this is the 'fruit of his Spirit'!"—Lise spoke the word with ironic bitterness. "His favorite verse in the whole of the New Testament is from Galatians: 'the fruit of the Spirit is love, joy, peace, patience, kindness, goodness, faithfulness, gentleness, self-control.' I couldn't begin to count the number of times I've heard him quote that, heard him preach on it, as though it were the measure by which he lived his life. I'm not sure he has ever known what love and kindness and goodness and gentleness mean. And now it seems that the fruit of his own spirit is bigotry and desperation and violence and death." And Lise broke down again in sobbing.

It was clear that, as tragic as she knew Rob Shaw's death to be on its own terms, this was for her life the larger tragedy.

Lane and Sandra waited out Lise's grief in silence. When once again she had regained her composure, Sandra said, "Lise, I want to make a suggestion. Don't contact your father now. Wait for his visit the day after tomorrow. Even if his prospective announcement is postponed as inappropriate under the circumstances, I suspect he will come. This is a moment of crisis for the College, and as the Board's chairman I feel certain he'll want to be here.

"There are a couple of reasons for waiting," said Sandra. "One is that you will want to come to a clearer sense of just what it is you want to say to him. Why don't you come to my office tomorrow afternoon, as we've planned. We can talk about that.

"The other reason," Sandra added, "is that it's just possible your father will have some feelings of his own to come to terms with, possibly even some feelings of responsibility to face, some assessing, perhaps even reassessing to do. I'd give him some time. The next forty-eight hours before you two meet may be important for both of you, in your own ways."

Lise nodded her agreement. "You're very wise," she said. "And I'm grateful to you both for your support and concern. You were here when I needed you."

So Lane drove Lise back to her campus dormitory. On the way he suggested that he pick her up for supper on the following evening, and told her to call him in the meantime if she simply wanted to talk. Lise accepted both suggestions with thanks.

As she left the car, she kissed him quickly on the cheek.

CHAPTER TWELVE

REASSESSMENTS

Lane Thomas was so distressed by the sad circumstance of the morning—and so exhilarated by Lise's departing kiss—that he almost forgot he was expected to meet Anne Armstrong and Jim Denison for lunch at the Towne Grill. It was already a few minutes past noon when he left Lise at the dormitory, so he drove directly to the restaurant.

It would certainly be a different conversation from the one the three had anticipated when they made the agreement two days before, he thought. Surely Anne and Jim would have heard by now of Rob Shaw's death and of the note he left explaining it. That was likely to change everything. The President and the Trustees couldn't possibly go through with the planned announcement on Friday—or could they?

Lane found Anne and Jim at a table near the back of the restaurant. Lane had barely seated himself when Jim said, without preliminary, "God, I feel responsible for Rob's death!"

Anne and Lane looked startled, and Anne said, "Are you the one who told the students about the new policy?"

"No, no," said Jim, "that's not it. It was something I said in a telephone conversation with Lane last Saturday morning—you know, the morning after. I said that being required to suppress one's true self is disastrous. And then I said—I remembered so clearly saying it when I heard about Rob this morning—and then I said, 'I'm surprised we haven't had a student suicide already.' It's almost as if I evoked it, willed it, to prove how awful bigotry is. God, it is awful. Poor Rob! For that matter, poor Macauley College!"

Anne and Lane wanted to persuade Denison that he had played no role in the tragedy of the morning, but Denison wasn't to be put off with glib reassurances. "I know," he said, "that there's no direct thread tying me to what happened. But it's just too damned easy to blame Charlie Kean and the Board, as if they bear sole responsibility for it. God knows I do blame them. And that faculty bastard, whoever he is, who passed on the information that got to Rob. I blame him, too, and I hope he's suffering for it. If he had kept his mouth shut, we might have been able to prevent the making of the announcement, and this thing would never have happened.

"But I blame the rest of us, too. We've permitted Charlie Kean and his minions, with their narrow and bigoted brand of religious literalism, to run rough-shod over the humane traditions of this place. We've griped privately, but until now we've not uttered a single public word against it. Why? Because they promised to bring us more students and more funding, and that translates into greater faculty job security and higher salaries, humane traditions be damned!

"As old Hosea said, we sowed the wind, and now we've reaped the whirlwind." Jim Denison leaned back in his booth seat, emotionally drained by the accumulation of two hours of brooding over Rob Shaw's death.

No one spoke for a time. A server, seeing no activity at the table and thinking they might be waiting for her, came over and asked if they were ready to order. None of them felt much like eating, but since they were occupying a restaurant table, ordering seemed the appropriate thing to do, so they went with soup and salads again.

When the server had gone, Jim Denison said to Lane, "By the way, I've invited Morton Emmons to join us at 12:30. Anne already knows that he's decided to go public in opposition to Kean and Warner, so I thought we should bring him into our conversations. I left a message for you this morning, but you didn't return my call."

Lane apologized but didn't explain the compromising reason for his distraction, and Denison proceeded to tell them both more fully about his conversation with the Dean.

"Of course," said Jim, "the whole strategy has to be rethought now, in the light of Rob Shaw's death. But I think we should defer that conversation until Morton is here." They agreed.

Dean Emmons arrived just as their lunch orders were being served, and as he joined them he asked the server to bring him coffee.

Anne said to Emmons, "Morton, we're very grateful for your decision to oppose the President and the Board. In retrospect, it's not surprising, since you've always acted on principle, but it simply didn't occur to us to go to you. Thanks for coming to us."

Emmons said, "Tell me how you think I can be of most help."

Anne said, "I've given some quick thought to this whole thing since the sad event of the morning, and I've had a very brief consultation with my Political Science colleagues and with the attorney in town. We think it's highly unlikely that Kean will go through with the announcement tomorrow morning. It would be a virtual public admission of institutional responsibility for Rob Shaw's death. But there's no guarantee that the policy may not be resurrected at some later time when this incident has been largely forgotten—or, what might be even worse, that, even without a formal policy, efforts will be made to identify allegedly homosexual students and action will be taken against them informally."

"I think you're exactly right on both counts," said Jim Denison. "Which says to me that our intervention is still needed." Lane and Morton Emmons nodded their agreement.

Morton added, "This morning I was given a copy of the note Rob Shaw left for his roommate. There's one aspect of it that may be important to what we plan in response. It's addressed to the roommate, Steve Braithwaite. I'll read it to you."

He took out the document and began to read:

Dear Steve:

I apologize for putting you through this, but I can't face what seems to be in front of me. Since my last year in high school, I've known that I'm gay. I couldn't even let you know that, close as we were, because of my deep shame. Now it seems unlikely that I could keep it from the college authorities for very much longer, and I'm terribly afraid that,

*when it becomes known, it will jeopardize my chance for graduation
and for getting into law school, which is the only thing I've ever
wanted to do with my life. I just can't deal with the pain of my own
disappointed hopes and with disgrace that would come my family. Tell
my parents that I love them. I love you, too. Forgive me for leaving
you with this mess.*

Rob

"What an awful thing!" said Lane. "He must have been in absolute agony."

"Notice," said Morton Emmons, "that he doesn't directly mention the threatened Trustee policy, though when you know about it, the presence of that threat is clear enough just below the surface. The point is that when the administration releases the note, as it's likely to do to explain the death, it will not be implicated directly."

"Then," said Anne, "here's what I think we should do. While the administration is feeling vulnerable, someone—Morton, here, would be ideal—should go to Kean on our behalf. In the event that the announcement is to be made as originally planned, he should know that we will proceed at once to our court filings.

"If the announcement is merely to be postponed, he should understand that we will be ready to file on the day it is made, whenever that may be.

"I think we should ask him for an on-the-spot assurance that he will not act against homosexual students, either formally or informally, now or in the future. If he refuses, I think he should be told that we will go public at once with the full story. He can't afford to appear to have triggered a student suicide."

"The situation for the administration is even more precarious than you know," said Morton Emmons. "Just before coming here, I learned that the source of the leak that reached Rob Shaw was Charles Kean himself!"

"So he's the bastard!" Jim Denison spat out the words. Anne and Lane greeted Emmons' information with astonished silence.

Emmons went on. "Kean apparently decided to ingratiate himself with Tim Considine, president of the Associated Students of Macauley College, since he knew that young Tory well and was certain that Tim would welcome news of the prospective new policy. Furthermore, although Charles expected little active opposition from within the student body, he wanted to prepare this well-placed young man to be his advocate and interpreter once the policy was announced.

"My own experience with Tim is that he couldn't keep a confidence if his life depended on it. As it turned out, Rob's life did. The rest, sadly, is known to us all.

"One more thing," Emmons added. "You may be surprised—I certainly have been—at the number of individual faculty members who have taken me aside to express dismay at the President's announcement, and to tell me they hoped something would be done to preempt it."

"Then the conditions for action are even more propitious than we thought," said Jim Denison. "And the ideal time to convey our message is Friday when John Warner is here. In fact, I think we should ask for a meeting with Warner and Kean together. It's important for the Board to know that some faculty members have no intention of giving in to their joint manipulations. And Morton, here, is the ideal person to carry that good news."

Anne said, "I've already asked our attorney to draw up a draft summons and complaint, which Morton can show to Kean and Warner as an earnest of our firm intent to act unless there is a satisfactory and clearly irreversible resolution of the issue in our favor," said Anne. "I can have the document in Morton's hands tomorrow morning."

Turning to Morton Emmons, Anne asked, "Are you willing to carry our message to Kean and Warner? Can you call the President today and ask for time on Friday morning to see the odious pair?"

"I am and I will!" he said with conviction.

"Meanwhile, we three have the rest of our day's work cut out for us," Anne said, addressing Jim and Lane. "We have individual lists of potential faculty supporters to compare. Then we'd better get on at once with contacting them."

Morton Emmons walked thoughtfully back to his campus office. He would telephone President Kean when he got there, but how would he explain a request to see Kean and Warner together on Friday morning? It would be unusual—even presumptuous—to request that the Chairman of the Board be included in their conversation, and it might signal more of the faculty conspirators' intent than was wise. Rather than giving Kean a chance to prepare, he wanted to retain some strategic element of preemptive surprise, and how he would manage that he wasn't at all sure. Well, he would just have to feel his way into the conversation, see what kind of an opening Kean might inadvertently provide.

Once in his office, he dialed the President's extension and announced himself to the secretary. When she had identified the caller to the President and put him through, Kean said without preliminary, "Bad business, Morton! Bad business! Young Shaw has certainly created some problems for us."

"Yes, well," Emmons began. He wanted to say that, on the contrary, it was the homophobic malice and egregious insensitivity of President and Board that had created the problems, but he'd hold that kind of language for the meeting he would propose for Friday. Instead he said, "It's a tragic waste."

"I've talked about it by telephone with John Warner, the Board chairman. Of course, we'll have to cancel the press-conference announcement for now," Kean went on without giving Emmons a chance to say why he was calling. "Have to try to avoid any major institutional embarrassment. See to damage control."

But the damage can't be controlled, Emmons thought bitterly. It's irreversible. Rob Shaw can't be brought back.

Charles Kean pressed on. "Shaw's parents are coming in tonight. I've asked the Chaplain and the Dean of Students to handle all of that. Hope I won't have to do much more than say 'Hello' and

'I'm sorry' to them.

"By the way," Kean continued, "I'm glad you called. I was going to try to reach you this afternoon. Even without the press conference, Dr. Warner is still planning to come on Friday so that we can do some reconnoitering, see how the land lies, run a few ideas up the pole, that sort of thing. I'd like you to join us, at least for part of our conversation, because I'm sure there will be some information I'll want you to convey to the faculty afterward. How about eleven o'clock?"

"I'll be there," said the Dean. See what kind of an opening Kean would inadvertently provide, indeed, Emmons thought as he hung up. If Charles Kean only knew!

THURSDAY

CHAPTER THIRTEEN
HARD QUESTIONS

The twenty-four hours between Rob Shaw's suicide on Wednesday and her scheduled Thursday appointment with Sandra Albright were difficult ones for Lise Warner.

Not that her classroom studies proved to be any distraction. Late on Wednesday afternoon, Academic Dean Morton Emmons had announced the suspension of classes for the balance of the week. Not that Lise lacked opportunities for guided venting of feelings about what had happened. The college Chaplain and staff members from the Dean of Students Office had moved into the dormitories to encourage the sharing of grief, and to be immediately available to individuals for whatever their needs might be.

Lise avoided these dorm gatherings—in fact, abandoned the residence hall entirely, to walk meditatively about the town and down along the river that bordered a nearby public park. She was sure that her feelings, her needs for clarity, were unlike anyone else's. They were too personal, too critically tied to who she was, who she intended to be at her depth, to discuss with anyone else, except for Sandra Albright and Lane Thomas. Most especially she could not, would not, reveal them to other students.

Rob's death note had raised in its most poignant form her own question to Sandra Albright: How does a woman know she's a lesbian? The note had raised it because it spoke with fatal eloquence about the possible consequences of being gay—its impact on one's sense of self, on family, on relationships beyond the telling. The questions went well beyond the "how does one know" to "what if I am?"

But even if she were not, Lise thought, there is another question that, for her, might be even worse. If, in fact, her father were responsible in some tangible way for the death of that kind, gentle, admirable young man who, until Wednesday morning, had been so full of life and promise: that was something else again! If that were the yield of his piety, it would be monstrous, and she wasn't sure she could ever manage that.

So at least the questions for her talk with Sandra Albright were clear. She wondered if there could possibly be any answers.

It was with some ambivalence, then, that Lise Warner approached Sandra Albright's study at All Souls Church on Thursday afternoon. She very much looked forward to seeing the older woman, whom she had come, quite quickly, to think of as a trusted friend. But she was apprehensive about the possible consequences of any serious exploration of the two issues that were before her.

Sandra opened the door at Lise's knock and gave her a warm hug. "How have you been doing since yesterday?" Sandra wanted to know. "I've been thinking of you a lot, and I was tempted to call. But I knew you would feel free to call me if you felt the need, and I thought you might just like to be left alone with your own feelings and thoughts."

"Thanks for both," said Lise, "your concern, and your willingness to let me come to terms with Rob's death and its immediate implications in my own way. With classes canceled, I've had time to do a good bit of walking, since the combination of solitude and physical activity, which I've always found to be a good way to scatter depression, really helps me get some things sorted out."

"And how have things fallen out, as you've thought about them?" Sandra asked.

Lise had decided what she wanted to say to Sandra. "It's very clear to me that the two issues are: one, Who is Lise Warner? and two, What is she to do about John Warner? I don't mean to distance myself from those two by putting them in the third person, because I don't, in fact, feel distant from them at all. Actually a little more distance might be a good thing. I have felt those two questions so intensely, so intimately, over the last twenty-four hours particularly, that I suspect a bit more perspective will be useful."

"And what have you thought about those questions?" Sandra wanted to know.

"For one thing, that in the end they are really one question," said Lise. "I knew, of course, that they were connected. I told you, when we had lunch together on Monday, that I refused merely to give in mindlessly to becoming the person my father wants me to be. But Rob's death sharpened the connection for me.

"It forced the identity issue for me by the tragic acknowledgement of his own gayness. It made me realize that, until now, I haven't known who I am, what I am. And it sharpened my sense of alienation from my father because I realized that, if I were gay, I would be under his pitiless judgment just as Rob and others like him are.

"So for me there's nothing abstract, either in Rob's death or in the proposed anti-homosexual policy my father has conspired in. They are both about me!"

A few days ago, such a recital might have been accompanied by tears, as much the evidence of muddled feelings and thoughts as of anything else. Now there was only calm statement from one who really had come clear on what the questions were. Tears were likely to come later, the price of confronting hard answers.

Sandra responded. "Even though you've come to experience their interconnectedness, it may make things more manageable if we take each of the two questions separately. Is that acceptable to you?"

Lise said eagerly that it was.

"So, then," Sandra continued, "suppose we look at the question you asked me on Monday: 'How does a woman know she's a lesbian?' I don't want to play the coy therapist, because I sense that you have a need to come to terms fairly quickly with some aspects of your two questions. We can tease out the fine details at leisure later on. But let me be quite direct now and tell you that, from being with you, my feeling is that you are not a lesbian. That's largely an intuition, but it has usually proved pretty reliable. Reliable but far from infallible, so if you should conclude later that I'm wrong, you will have my full support and encouragement, as I hope you know. But you're not likely to need it.

"I can understand why you might wonder," Sandra went on. "There's no doubt that, because of the restrictions your family imposed earlier on your social activities during the high school years, you had only a limited opportunity to test your relationships with the opposite sex. And, having accepted that limitation, having become comfortable with it because of a long-standing habit of pleasing your parents and of conforming to their expectations of you, until now you simply haven't felt a strong yearning for male companionship. Have I made a reasonable guess?"

"More than reasonable," Lise replied. "There's no question that you are describing me."

"Okay," said Sandra, "let me tell you what else I sense. I'm willing to guess that, while you have probably had some close female friendships, you don't necessarily prefer the company of women, and that you are not uncomfortable in the company of men. I'm even willing to guess, without concrete evidence, that while you probably have never been touched intimately by a man, you are not uncomfortable with a man's more casual touch. Am I correct?"

"Right again," said Lise. "Yesterday when I reported to Dr. Thomas what the students in the coffee shop had told me about Rob Shaw, he hugged me—which is exactly what I wanted him to do. I guess I can tell you this, though it shocks me a bit to realize that I feel this way. I wanted him to keep on hugging me. I think he's the most attractive man I've ever met—his imagination, his unpretentiousness, his caring, his strength. I sit in his classes and fantasize about what it would be like to love a man like that, to be loved by a man like that, and frankly I like the way my fantasies feel. I've even dreamed about it."

"I rest my case," said Sandra. "At least, I do for the time being. We can go more deeply into all of these things later, if you want to. But I think this is a good beginning, particularly if it feels right to you."

"It does," Lise replied confidently.

"The issue around your anger with your father is much harder," Sandra went on. "And while there are probably some things we can say about it this afternoon in preparation for your talk with him tomorrow, I suspect it will take much longer for us to begin to get to the deep places.

"You may or may not want to do that, because getting to the deep places is often painful and upsetting and could involve more emotional cost than you are willing to expend. But there's no need for you to make a decision about that now.

"However," Sandra went on, "where anger is involved, there is another decision that has to come pretty early in the process. In fact, if you were able to make this decision now, at least provisionally, it would make a difference to what you might decide to say to your father tomorrow."

"Tell me," said Lise. "I'd like at least to give it a try. What do I have to do?"

Sandra said, "You have to ask yourself these questions: How important is it for me to hold on to my anger with him? How valuable is my resentment, my feeling of being victimized by him? How much satisfaction do I get from wounded pride, from feeling superior to my father's moral obtuseness?"

Lise was stunned by Sandra's questions, and for a moment she made no response. Then she said slowly, "I've never thought about it in that way. You're right, of course, that I do have those feelings: resentment, victimization, wounded pride, superiority. They have been among my most familiar emotions, especially since I left home to come to college and have been able to get enough emotional distance from my parents to be able to admit that I have such feelings.

"But the idea that I may have found some satisfaction in them, that I may have some emotional investment in them, and that I might therefore want to preserve them—that's something I have never even remotely considered."

"Do you think such a thing is likely?" Sandra wanted to know.

"I mean, that there is a place in you that values and wants to protect those feelings?"

Again Lise was silent for a time, turning over what was for her a radically new possibility, perhaps even a new truth about herself. "Yes," she said reflectively, "yes, I think it's more than likely."

"And how do you feel about that more-than-likelihood?" Sandra pressed gently.

"I don't like it," Lise said, more quickly this time. "I don't like the idea that my own self-esteem might be built on—what would you call it, invidious comparison? That valuing my own selfhood depended on devaluing another self? I don't like that at all!"

"That you don't feel a need to protect your investment in those negative feelings is a significant decision to arrive at, Lise. But it's not necessary for you to blame yourself for having had such feelings in order to balance the blame you have been assigning to someone else—in this case, to your father.

"It may take a while, but it will be important for you simply to be able to acknowledge to yourself that there is perfectly good reason for your anger, but that you don't intend to continue the victimization by giving that anger control of your life. Your acknowledgement of the legitimacy of your anger is essential to the process of letting it go."

Sandra let Lise have her silence for a space. And then Sandra said, even more gently, "There's something else—and it may be the hardest of all."

"I think I know," said Lise. "It has to do with telling my father directly about my anger, my resentment, my refusal to be his clone and my insistence on being my own person. Is that it?"

"Yes," Sandra said simply, and again let silence do its work.

Finally Sandra intervened. "You see, if you really decide both to acknowledge your anger and to give it up, that will free you, calm you, steady you for a less defensive, clearer, more authentic telling of how things really are with you—telling him not only of your anger with him, but of your love for him.

"And it may free him for a less defensive, clearer, more authentic hearing and responding."

"I see that," said Lise. "I'm not sure whether or not I can bring it off, but I see it and I want it."

"One other thing," said Sandra soberly, "and it's an important thing. I said that if you are able to approach your father in this way, it may free him to hear you in a new way—in fact, to discover a new you. But it may not. And you need to be prepared for that possibility. He may not be able, at least without some time and practice of his own, to get over his own investment in the kind of behavior that has angered you. That would be sad, of course; that would be cause for you to grieve. But at least you would have freed yourself from being its prisoner. And unlike resentment, grief can be a healing thing."

Lise rose from her chair and approached Sandra with her arms extended. They embraced for several minutes. There were tears on the faces of both women.

*

Lane Thomas had made a supper reservation for Lise and himself at the Stillwater Inn, a pleasant riverside restaurant ten miles outside of town. He told himself that it would provide a quieter setting for conversation than restaurants in the city, which was true. It was also true that he wanted a place where their being together was less likely to be noticed by people from the college.

For the same reason, he had arranged to pick Lise up at 6:30 p.m. at the curb near the entrance of her dormitory, rather than coming in to announce himself at the desk and call her down from her room, like an undergraduate date.

In his eagerness, he was at least ten minutes early at curbside, and he was pleasantly surprised to find that she was already waiting, just inside the dormitory entrance, for the appearance of his car. Was she eager too, he wondered, or merely punctilious? He thought his question was answered when, having gotten into the car beside him, she reached over and gave him the same kind of quick kiss on the cheek with which she had left him the previous afternoon.

As they drove out of town, they talked of the events that had absorbed them in the hours since the discovery of Rob Shaw's body on Wednesday morning. Although it was clear that each of them was still living within the reverberations of that awful discovery, each was now able to talk about it without the emotional intensity of the previous day.

"How do you think students generally are responding?" Lane asked.

"I'm not sure I can tell you very accurately," Lise replied. "I've kept pretty much to myself, trying to think my way through the personal implications this whole thing has had for me. But I've eaten my meals in the dining hall as usual, and I've picked up some impressions there—threads of conversation, nothing very sustained."

"What have you been hearing?" Lane wanted to know.

"Homosexuality wasn't much talked about among students before this happened. If you had asked me earlier how they stood on the issue, I would have said that in general there was a latent hostility toward gays. Nothing really overt, but a kind of homophobic undercurrent. It was largely abstract, I think—not based on firsthand acquaintance. On the whole not very thoughtful. Borrowed impressions and prejudices, I would have said. And I've never heard anyone, man or woman, on this campus rumored to be gay.

"But Rob Shaw—well, that's something else again. Rob was able to bridge the usual gap between the jocks and the non-jocks. He was a superior athlete and a superior student. Everybody liked him—I mean, everybody. So. Rob Shaw gay? For lots of people, Rob has put a different face on the issue."

"What had been your own feelings about homosexuality?" Lane asked.

"No more thoughtful than the people I've just been describing," she said with attractive candor. "The issue simply never came up in my circle of acquaintance. The only difference was that I had no negative feelings about it. I just didn't think about it one way or the other.

"Not until I met Sandra Albright, that is," Lise went on. "And when I saw what a warm, bright, attractive, empathic, wholly admirable person she is, suddenly I could even imagine myself as lesbian—though that was abstract too, since I had no realistic idea of what it would have meant to be one."

"How do you think students will react if the Trustees' policy against homosexuality should be announced, if not tomorrow then at some time in the near future?" Lane pressed.

"Do you think it will be?" Lise wanted to know, ignoring Lane's question.

"We're fairly certain that there won't be an announcement tomorrow. It would be in incredibly bad taste, with Rob so lately dead. And the administration will want to avoid even the slightest implication that something it did, or at least planned to do, had any connection with Rob's death. I think your father is coming in, not for an announcement but for a strategy session with President Kean."

"Yes, well, I want to talk with you about that," Lise said with new firmness in her voice.

"We're nearly at the restaurant," Lane observed. "Let's wait until we get there and have our dinners ordered. Then our conversation won't be interrupted."

Once inside the Stillwater Inn, they were seated at Lane's request in a quiet corner of the room, scanned the menus, ordered, and settled down for leisurely conversation.

"So," said Lane, "I can understand that you've been thinking a lot about what you may want to say to your father tomorrow. I assume you may have talked with Sandra about it this afternoon."

"Actually," said Lise, "we talked not so much about what I will say as about the way I'll try to say it. And I feel quite comfortable with that. I'm less sure, though, of what it is exactly that I am going to say. One thing I'm clear about, and that is that it can't all be said tomorrow. This is going to have to be the first of a series of conversations—unless he's totally unwilling to listen. At some point they will have to include my mother, either separately or with him. So I'm concentrating specifically on what I most want to tell him now."

"Obviously I can't tell you what to say," Lane responded, "and I'm sure you wouldn't want me to. But maybe I can help you clarify some things. What do you want him to know? What's uppermost in your mind?"

Lise seemed to be in no doubt about that. She said at once and with some intensity, "I want him to know that I consider the proposed anti-homosexual policy to be totally unacceptable by any humane standard—indeed by any Christian standard; and that I am embarrassed, disappointed, and angry that he has had a major hand in bringing it about. Most of all, I want him to understand what I consider to be his own personal responsibility for Rob's death. And I want him to know that I intend to take a very public position in opposing the proposed policy, should he, the Board, and the President be determined to see it through, either now or in the future."

"You do know what you want to say!" Lane said, admiringly.

"I guess I do," she replied with a note of surprise in her voice, "but I didn't really know it until I said it."

"Dr. Thomas," Lise went on, but Lane stopped her. "Please," he said, "call me Lane. Outside of class, I hope we can just be good friends."

Lise said shyly, "Thanks. I'd like that." And then she continued, "What I'd like to know is whether or not the faculty is going to let the administration get away with eliminating gays from the student body?"

"There's probably a division among the faculty, as among the students," said Lane. "Some, I regret to say, will be active supporters of the proposed policy. Some won't favor it but won't actively oppose it. But we have reason to think that a substantial number are in opposition.

"I'm not free to give you all of the details or to tell you who the actors are. But because I trust you, I can tell you in confidence that there is a group of faculty who will ask the Superior Court to issue an injunction against the policy, on the ground that the Trustee failure to consult the faculty constituted a breach of contract.

"There is also the possibility that a suit may be brought in Federal District Court asking an injunction on behalf of students, on the ground that the policy would violate their civil rights. But we would have to find a student—probably someone who is willing to admit to being gay—to be the plaintiff in a class action on behalf of other potentially aggrieved students, and that seems pretty problematic at the moment.

"In any event," Lane continued, "by the time you meet your father for lunch tomorrow, he and President Kean will have been informed of these two prospective actions and will have been given an opportunity to renounce the policy permanently."

"I'm immensely relieved to know that there's going to be some organized resistance," Lise said, and her manner showed that relief. "Together we may just be able to turn this awful thing back," she added brightly.

Lane took her brightness as an opportunity to turn the conversation to other things. The transition was aided by the arrival of their food.

When the waitress had left, Lane said, "You know, yesterday you told me that teachers have the advantage of knowing more about students than students know about teachers. But in fact there are lots of things about you that I don't know, that I want very much to know. About your aspirations, your dreams."

"I'd be embarrassed to tell you about my dreams," Lise said, lowering her eyes and her voice provocatively. "But what can I tell you?"

"Everything!" said Lane. "Tell me everything that comes to your mind."

So she did. They both did. They talked on spontaneously, enthusiastically, warmly, intimately, as if they had known each other forever.

Finally, aware of a sudden increase in activity around them, they realized that the restaurant was preparing to close and that the hour was approaching ten. "I suppose we should head back to the campus," Lane said, regret in his voice.

"At least, with classes canceled, we don't have to face each other, bleary-eyed, at eight o'clock tomorrow morning." said Lise.

"I've noticed that you manage to look lovely even at that unlikely hour of the day," Lane rejoined.

"Thank you, kind sir," said Lise, with genuine pleasure beneath her mock coyness.

Lane paid the check and they headed for the car. In contrast to their active talk at the table, neither spoke on the drive back to town. It was not an uneasy silence, but the silence of two people who are entirely at ease with each other. Midway through, Lane moved his hand on the seat tentatively toward Lise. He found her hand there waiting for him.

Rather than pulling up directly in front of the dormitory entrance, Lane stopped in a shadow a bit farther up the block. "I'm really not ready for this to end," he told her.

"Neither am I," she said.

He wanted to take her in his arms, to kiss her, but he feared that might be rushing things. Instead, he put her hand to his lips and kissed her fingers. Slowly she withdrew her hand, kissed her own fingers, and placed them on his lips. Then she slipped out of the car without saying a word.

FRIDAY

CHAPTER FOURTEEN

CONFRONTATIONS

It was five minutes past eleven when Morris Emmons was shown into President Kean's office. John Warner had not yet arrived, although he had been expected at ten o'clock for a preliminary conversation with the President. Warner had called Kean at home before eight o'clock to say that a pastoral emergency had delayed him, but that he was now on his way and would likely arrive by 11.

Emmons and Kean had barely exchanged greetings when John Warner came bustling in, all effusiveness for his late arrival and repeating his "pastoral emergency" explanation.

"I believe you gentlemen know each other," the President said breezily. They acknowledged that to be true and shook hands.

John Warner cut an impressive figure. Tall, hair graying at 50, his frame somewhat stocky but trim, his dress was conservative and impeccable, with crisp white shirt, regimental-striped tie, and dark suit. "Substantial" was a word that came to mind, as Morton Emmons surveyed him. Except for his pastoral manner—oiliness was the way Emmons thought of it—Warner would more likely be taken for a corporate executive than for a clergyman.

In fact, he looked more presidential than Charles Kean, Emmons thought. Kean's 5'10" frame was undisciplined, and he had affected a rather rumpled style, on the assumption that it was more collegiate and would help to persuade campus people that he really belonged there. Instead, it merely gave them something else to caricature.

Did John Warner aspire to become Macauley's president, Emmons wondered? Might he be some day? Emmons shuddered inwardly at the thought. Although he had not had frequent contact with Warner, he had never liked the Board chairman. There was something too mannered, too measured, too well modulated about his style. It was impossible to tell what was really going on behind those cold blue eyes. But Emmons reflected, with satisfaction, that he would be retired and long gone before any such presidential aspiration could come to pass.

The three sat down in front of a fireplace that was ablaze with fresh logs. "Thanks for coming. We've got a lot of heavy stuff to digest, so let's step right up to the plate," Kean said, with his usual gift for metaphor. "Obviously we've got a very difficult P.R. problem on our hands, and we've got to try to hit one over the fence. What I want to suggest is—"

"Excuse me, Charles," Morton Emmons interrupted. "I think you and Dr. Warner may want to hear what I have to say before the conversation goes any farther."

"What you have to say?" Kean rejoined brusquely, not pleased by the interruption. "It was I who invited you to this meeting."

"Yes," said Emmons, not intimidated by Kean's tone, "but I think you will be well-advised to hear me out. It may save you a great deal of time, and I think it may also save you from a quite a lot of inconvenience and embarrassment."

"Perhaps we'd better hear the Dean out," said John Warner evenly. "Sounds rather serious."

Emmons drew a document from an inner pocket and handed a copy to each of the men. "This is the draft of a petition to the Superior Court, requesting an injunction against the President and Board of Trustees of Macauley College, to prevent the enforcement of a policy banning homosexuals from the College student body. I am named as the plaintiff in this class-action suit on behalf of members of the College faculty. We claim in the petition that when the Board failed to consult the faculty before promulgating its anti-homosexual policy, it breached its contract with the faculty."

Kean, getting up from his chair, sputtered almost uncontrollably. "This—this is—this is outrageous," he finally managed to say. "I've—I've never heard of such arrogant presumption. How dare you!"

"No, Charles," Emmons said calmly. "The shoe is on the other foot. We are saying, How dare you! The policy you and the Board propose is both legally flawed and ethically reprehensible, and we don't intend to stand idly by while you trash the humane traditions of this institution. And while I have scant standing for saying so, in my judgment the proposed policy mocks the Christian profession of the College. You need to know that there is broad-based support within the faculty for action to prevent its implementation.

"Moreover," Emmons went on, "you also need to know that I have in hand the draft of a petition for filing in the U.S. District Court—a class action suit on behalf of the students of Macauley College—asking an injunction against the same policy on the ground that it will violate student civil rights. It will name a student as plaintiff."

Now Charles Kean was almost apoplectic, and he looked as if he were about to have a stroke. John Warner intervened. "Sit down, Charles, please. Let's see if we can discuss this calmly. Let's see if we can understand what's going on."

Kean sat, and John Warner took over the direction of the meeting. "Let me see if I understand you," he said to Morton Emmons. "You and your faculty colleagues are alleging that failure to consult you on this policy issue represents a breach of contract? How so?"

Emmons took a copy of the Macauley catalog from the coffee table in front of them and handed it to Warner. "Have a look at page 3," he said. "You will find there the statement of educational purpose of the College. It is, in effect, a *de facto* contract with parents, students, and teachers specifying the kind of wholistic learning experience they can expect to find here.

"When we interview prospective teachers, we always discuss this statement with them. We probe their willingness to be engaged with students outside of the classroom. I wish they were more conscientious about that once they're appointed, but we set the expectation and thereby create an implied contract.

"We even have what are called 'Seminar Homes,' College-owned residences rented by faculty members with the understanding that they will conduct seminars and entertain students in those homes, as an effort to create a more wholistic relationship between teachers and students.

"You know, I am sure," Emmons went on, "that the official Handbook of the College gives to the faculty primary responsibility for initiating and establishing educational policy, subject of course to Trustee review. I think you will find, from the statements on page 3, that personal learnings of students are considered to be an integral part of Macauley's educational intent, its educational policy, and as such fall properly within the purview of the faculty.

"The Trustees' recent failure to respect that purview represents breach of contract, as we are prepared to explain in Superior Court.

"I assume that I don't have to tell you what is at issue in asking the Federal Court for an injunction on civil rights grounds."

John Warner looked at Charles Kean. "What are we to say to the Dean," he asked. "His challenge is obviously serious."

The President was inclined to bluster. "I say he can go to hell," said Kean, "and take his class action with him!"

"There's one other thing," said Emmons, addressing Kean directly. "We know that you violated your own insistence, in last week's faculty meeting, on confidentiality regarding the prospective new policy until it could be announced by Dr. Warner today. We know that you gave advanced information about the policy to student body president Tim Considine, that Tim shared the information with other students, that it eventually reached Rob Shaw, and that your breach of confidentiality was the circumstance that led directly to Shaw's suicide.

"There may not be a basis for legal liability, but there can be no question of your moral liability. Speaking of 'a difficult P.R. problem,' I think the campus, and indeed the community at large, would be shocked if that information got out."

Again John Warner looked at Charles Kean, and this time his look seemed to say, You really are an idiot! Kean appeared entirely demoralized and unable to form any articulate response.

So John Warner said to Morton Emmons, "What do you and your colleagues want?"

"We want respect for our own contractual prerogatives, and humane consideration for our students. More specifically, we want assurance on two points: one, that you will not go forward with the formal policy; and two, that the College will not seek out and act against homosexual students as a matter of informal policy, either now or in the future.

"We are prepared to wait until Monday for your response. If we have not heard from you by noon on that day, we will make President Kean's indiscretion known publicly. Should you decide to go forward with the anti-homosexual policy at any time, however soon or late, we will file the legal briefs as of that instant."

"You drive a hard bargain," Warner said to Emmons.

"You made an egregious miscalculation," said Emmons in response.

When Morton Emmons had left, a very sober John Warner said to Charles Kean, "I don't want to go into this further right now. I need to do some thinking about it. Besides, I have a lunch date with my daughter. You're obviously in no condition to talk constructively now anyway. You think about it over the noon hour. We'll talk when I come back around 1:30."

And he left without a word from Charles Kean.

*

John Warner had made a reservation for lunch for himself and Lise at the Olmsted Park Hotel, where he thought there would be less noise and confusion than he had found on earlier occasions at the Towne Grill. Since it was only eight short blocks from the campus, Lise had proposed to walk and meet him there at 12:30.

She had arrived early and was already seated at their table when he entered the dining room. He had a broad smile of greeting. She rose to accept the standard paternal hug, a rather stiff performance, and noted how different it felt from the more yielding embraces of

Lane Thomas.

"So," said John Warner, "how are you. I'm glad to see you. Your mother sends love, of course. Wishes she could have come along."

"How is she?" Lise wanted to know.

"Well and happy as always," said her father. Lise wondered about the accuracy of that report, but reflected that if her mother were otherwise, her father would be the last to know.

"My time is somewhat limited," he said. "I have to go back to the President's office for another meeting after lunch. I assume you've looked at the menu, so let's order right away. Then we'll have time to talk."

He signaled to the server, who came quickly over, took their orders efficiently, and disappeared into the kitchen.

"You look troubled," he said to Lise. "Is anything wrong?"

Lise was surprised that he had noticed. "Very wrong," she said, and he was startled at the strength and tone of her words. "You know about Rob Shaw's death, of course."

"Of course," he said gently. "Did you know him?"

"I wonder that you didn't call me when it happened to find out," said Lise firmly, determined not to cry. "Everybody knew him. But his death was, for me, the most incredibly sad thing that has ever happened in my very protected life, and it has brought about a major change in the way I think about myself—and the way I think about you. And what makes it so especially sad for me is that I know it was preventable—that you could have prevented it."

This was a Lise whom John Warner had never known before. She had always been such a submissive child. This note of challenge was quite new. He wasn't sure what to do with her, so he thought that he had better hear more before he decided how to respond.

"I don't quite understand," he said. "How could I have prevented Rob Shaw's death?"

"By not leading the Trustees in endorsing an anti-homosexual policy in the first place," she said. "Surely you know it was the prospect of that policy which, in effect, condemned Rob to death—led directly to his death, at the very least."

"I think you put it a bit strongly," said John Warner. "I have been told that a rumor of such a policy circulated among some of the students prior to Rob's taking of his own life. I've also been told that despair over the prospect of such a policy motivated his action, although the note he left makes no specific mention of it. But nobody condemned him to death, least of all myself. He made that choice quite freely, however tragic a choice it may have been,"

"I'm afraid," Lise responded firmly, "that your disavowal is much too easy, as though you have not been directly responsible for creating the climate of fear within which Rob did what he did—felt driven to do what he did. The policy you helped to create was both mischievous and cruel. And I have to tell you that I am embarrassed, I am angry, I am hurt that it was my father who helped set the whole sad sequence in motion."

For years John Warner had practiced and perfected a style of pastoral self-restraint, suppressing his own feelings in order to deal evenly with a hurt and angry parishioner. But he had had no practice in responding that way to his daughter.

Wanting to strike a conciliatory note without yielding his dominant position, he said, "I hear your pain, and I'm genuinely sorry that you have such strong feelings. But I'm afraid you don't understand about homosexuality. It's not just a casual social option that could as easily be one way as the other. It's a sin. And we wouldn't be acting as responsible Christians in a Christian college if we didn't make its sinful character known—if we didn't attempt to root it out, to protect the unsuspecting from its ungodly influence."

"And homophobia is not a sin, is that what you're telling me?" Lise responded. "Sitting in peremptory judgment on the life of another human being is not a sin? The policy proposed to expel a student merely for acknowledging his homosexuality, even if he didn't practice it. So punishing a person not for what he does but for what he thinks, for what he feels, is not a sin? Is that what you're telling me?" Lise retorted.

"Don't condescend to me, Father. I'm no longer a child. Don't tell me I don't understand. I understand only too well. You think being a Christian is simple because you've made up your own yesses and noes. Well, there's nothing simple about compassion. There's nothing simple about reconciliation. They take imagination, and they have to be re-imagined for every person we meet.

"You may think I haven't read the New Testament, but I have. I've read all of it since coming to Macauley. I've thought about it a lot. And I don't think Jesus would be proud of your role in this tragic business."

John Warner was stunned into silence, but Lise wasn't finished.

"Let me tell you how strongly I feel about your anti-homosexual policy. If you and the President and the Trustees decide to go through with it, I will publicly declare myself a lesbian and ask to be named the plaintiff in a class-action suit claiming violation of student civil rights."

Neither father nor daughter spoke for several minutes as both absorbed the import of what had happened between them. Then Lise said, her tone gentler now, "It's essential for me to tell you one other thing. I said that I am embarrassed, angry, and hurt because of what you have proposed to do—have in fact done—here. I am. But I also love you as my father. Disappointment doesn't begin to exhaust the depth of my feeling for you, my gratitude for many good things you've given me.

"And if you should be surprised at my present intensity, you need to know that this anger is not merely for what has happened in recent days. It goes back a very long way, and at some point—not today, because these immediate feelings must be attended to now—but at some point I want to tell you about my larger, longer anger. Perhaps you will let me know when—if—you're ready to hear it.

"Meanwhile," she concluded, "I hope you'll reconsider what you and the Trustees have proposed to do."

Now Warner was not merely stunned but shaken. Who was

this person who sat across the table from him? How had she developed from a submissive, innocent child into a woman who could speak feelingly of love and of anger? Where had he been while she was growing the strength to stand independently for what she believed? How had he missed out on it all?

He said, "Thank you for telling me these things now."

They ate in silence for a time, and then John Warner said, "I can't say at the moment exactly what I'm going to do with what you've told me, but I can say that I have heard you very clearly.

"And that I love you."

*

Back in Charles Kean's office at 1:30, Warner found the President in a state of deep depression, still slumped in a large upholstered chair before the now-dying fire. Warner said, "I'm going home. My advice to you—no, my instruction to you—is to keep your head down for the next couple of days. In fact, I want you to hole up for the weekend. You've created enough of a problem for us by your indiscretion with Tim Considine. Don't see anybody unless you absolutely have to. I want to think through what has to be done under the circumstances, maybe consult with a few key Board members. I'll be back in touch with you not later than the first thing on Monday morning, so that we can make a response to Morton Emmons's crowd by noon. If something really important happens, call me, but I'll hope not to hear from you. Is that clear?"

Kean's response was no more than a confirming groan from the depths of the enveloping chair.

*

When Morton Emmons had left Charles Kean and John Warner in the President's office, he returned to his own office and immediately attempted to call Anne Armstrong, Lane Thomas, and Jim Denison to give them an account of the meeting. Finding none of them in, he left voice-mail messages detailing the confrontation—reporting on Kean's emotional collapse and on Warner's coolly-noncommital demeanor.

Emmons told his co-conspirators that, rather than demanding an immediate cease-and-desist commitment from Kean and Warner—a demand he had concluded would probably be counter-productive—he had thought it wiser to give them time to reconsider, if reconsideration were at all in their repertoire. So he had set a deadline of Monday noon for their response. He had no way of guessing what they would do, he said, but he was sure they considered the threatened faculty action entirely credible, fully serious.

Emmons proposed to contact the President at noon on Monday, and suggested that the four of them meet again at the Towne Grill at 12:45 on Monday afternoon for a situation appraisal.

He said he hoped they'd have a relaxing weekend anyway!

SUNDAY

CHAPTER FIFTEEN

ANOTHER UNUSUAL SUNDAY

Lane Thomas was enormously curious about the outcome of Lise Warner's lunch-time meeting with her father, so he called her at her dormitory residence on Friday night to inquire. But he wanted to know more than she could tell him on the telephone, and besides, he didn't want a lengthy conversation on personal matters to raise any suspicions in the mind of Lise's roommate.

More than that, he simply wanted to see her again. Impatient, but apprehensive that he might appear to Lise to be moving more quickly than she would welcome, he thought it wise to let a couple of days intervene before proposing to meet her.

"Are you likely to be at All Souls on Sunday morning?" he asked.

"More than likely," she replied. "I want to be there, partly just to have another occasion to see Sandra."

"How about meeting me at the coffee hour following the service," Lane proposed. "I'll fix brunch for us at my house, if that's acceptable to you. That way we can talk as long as we like and in complete confidence, without having serving people hovering about, or others at adjacent tables to overhear."

True as that was, he knew it was only part of the real reason. As on Friday night, the larger truth was that he simply wanted to have Lise entirely to himself, quite out of public view.

Lise seemed to have no reluctance in accepting his invitation. In fact, he thought there was a note of eagerness in her voice. And then she told him briefly about the encounter with her father, indicating that its outcome was as yet uncertain, and promising a fuller account on Sunday.

On Sunday morning, when Lane arrived at the church a few minutes before the organ prelude began, he looked around for Lise, but either she hadn't yet appeared or she was blocked from his sight in pews that were already almost full. No matter, since the arrangement was for them to meet at the conclusion of the service.

On this particularly Sunday morning, the preacher was to be the Rev. Dr. Cameron Chase, with Sandra Albright as the liturgist. Cam Chase was completing a decade as rector of All Souls, after an earlier ten years during which he had been the chaplain of an Episcopal prep school in New England and had earned a Doctor of Ministry degree at Andover Newton Theological School, near Boston. He was regarded in the local community as its ablest preacher, and he continued to receive the occasional invitation to preach on the prep-school circuit, with Sandra Albright in the pulpit on the Sundays when Cam Chase was away.

When Lane attended worship, he usually sat on the pulpit side of the chancel, about a third of the way back and on the side aisle. It was close enough to the front to offer moral support to the preacher and worship leaders, far enough back to avoid any appearance of pious exhibitionism.

When Sandra Albright used an opening prayer she had selected from Frederick Buechner, novelist and theologian and a great favorite of Lane's, Lane had a strange sense that there might be, in this service, something more than ordinarily pointed toward his own life:

> *Lord, catch us off guard today. Surprise us with some moment of beauty or pain so that for at least a moment we may be startled into seeing that you are with us here in all your splendor, always and everywhere, barely hidden, beneath, beyond, within this life we breathe.*
>
> *When we meet as men and women, help us also to see beneath the differences of sex our common humanity, our common needs, so that we may love and serve each other fully. Open our hearts to the knowledge that beneath our hunger for one another lies a deeper hunger yet, a deeper emptiness which finally only you can fill. Open our hearts to the knowledge that we can be fully each other's only when we are fully*

yours. Amen.

"...beneath our hunger for one another lies a deeper hunger yet, a deeper emptiness...," said Buechner's prayer. Was "hunger" the right word to describe what he had been feeling for Lise? If so, was there more to that feeling than simple romantic attraction? Was it possible that Lise was only an occasion for the surfacing of something deeper, more enigmatic? Might his feelings for her be a symptom of emptiness, something profoundly missing in his own life? And if not, why had it occurred to him now, in this prayer spoken by Sandra, that it might be? She had surely not suggested it, had not called his name in the prayer. It was he who had made the connection, and he hadn't the least idea what to do with it.

Lane tried to put these questions out of his mind. But he was so absorbed in them that he didn't realize, at first, that he was the only one in the congregation who was sitting, while everyone around him had stood to sing a hymn.

Cameron Chase's sermon added to Lane's sense that, in some uncanny way, this service had been designed with him in mind. The sermon was entitled "Love's Other Abuse."

"These days a great deal of attention is being focused on egregious acts of physical violence that occur within intimate relationships," Chase said, *"and that is as it ought to be. There is no justification for such predations, and we ought to demand that they be stopped. If the victim cannot make that demand effectively, then a caring community—and most especially a caring Christian community—ought to make that demand in the victim's behalf.*

"Yet," said the preacher, *"there is in our relatedness a danger far more prevalent, far more subtle and insidious, far more common than physical violence. It is our manipulation of each other that we often disguise as love— disguise it from ourselves as well as from the other.*

"It is simply a fact, against which we must continually struggle," he said, *"that what begins as love, what touts itself proudly as love, often turns destructive. Love is readily and regularly confused with the attempted possession, the absorption, of one life by another. What justifies itself as humility and selflessness readily becomes the most subtle and dangerous form of ag-*

gression against another human being. What begins as service to another is often transformed by imperceptible degrees into condescension, manipulation, control.

"Such are the surface similarities between love and possession, between service and manipulation, and such is our talent for self-deception," said Chase, "that we easily persuade ourselves that we are engaged in the former while wreaking the spiritual havoc of the latter. Thus does love turn destructive, even demonic.

"But real love, whatever else it may be, is nothing less than the willingness to live in intimacy while permitting the other to be the other. Paradoxical as it may seem, if we are to find a capacity for loving intimacy, we shall have to maintain a certain loving distance from the beloved.

"There is more to intimacy than being close."

Lane didn't hear the rest of the sermon—indeed, wasn't aware of much of the rest of the service. He had already heard enough, wasn't sure he wanted to hear any more, and he brooded over its implications.

He was quite certain, of course, that Cameron Chase had described with telling accuracy the manipulative "love" John Warner had for his daughter. But putting prayer and sermon together, was it possible that Lane's own feelings for Lise were a form of manipulation, generated to fill an "emptiness," a "deep hunger" within his own life? Was it possible that what he had begun to feel for her might be an early form of affectional aggression that was more concerned about what those feelings could do for him, rather than for what they might do to her?

Suddenly he broke his brooding and said to himself, "No, damn it. That's not the way it is! I love her. More than that, I care about her, and I would never do anything to hurt her."

Misgivings resolved just in time, he stood to sing the closing hymn.

At the conclusion of the organ postlude—variations on a Bach chorale tune this time—he joined the throng of departing worshippers on their way to the coffee hour in Cranmer Hall. He spotted Lise, who was already there and was standing somewhat apart from the conversation clusters, the better to locate him when he walked in. Lane waved to her to stay where she was, and threaded his way through those clusters to join her.

"Hello!" he said. "It gave me a great feeling to look across the room, see you there, and know you were waiting for me. Would you like some coffee?"

"Not now," she said, putting her hand on his arm and giving it a welcoming squeeze. "I assume you'll be making some when we get to your house. I've already spoken to Sandra. Rather than sitting through the postlude, I came out to catch her before the general departure. She pulled me into her office and I had at least a brief time to tell her about meeting with my father. She and I are getting together tomorrow morning, and I'll fill her in on the details then.

"But I'd like to stay long enough now to thank Dr. Chase for his sermon. I can hardly believe it: a sermon worth hearing two Sundays in a row, first Sandra and now him. I could get used to this kind of thing!"

Lane didn't respond to her comment on the sermon, but he willingly followed Lise to the end of the line of half a dozen people waiting to speak with Cameron Chase. The line moved with reasonable speed, and when it was their turn, Lane said, "Cam, I'd like you to meet Lise Warner. From what she's just told me, she's an instant fan of yours."

Dr. Chase grasped Lise's hand warmly and said, "I'm really pleased to meet you. You must be the Comparative Literature person Sandra Albright has told me a bit about. I know how enthusiastic she is about you, and I look forward to knowing you, too."

Lise was startled—and complimented—to discover that Chase already knew her name and something about her from Sandra. "I want to thank you for 'Love's Other Abuse,'" she said. "You've helped me to understand the tragedy of misdirected love. I found my own experience reflected in what you said at a number of points. Your sermon today, and Sandra's last week, complement each other in a remarkable way. So I just wanted to say, Thanks!"

"I envy the contact Sandra has already had with you, and I hope there will be an early chance for you and me to get acquainted," Cameron Chase said in warm response.

Together Lise and Lane walked out of the church and into the bright midday crispness of a fine fall Sunday. They got into Lane's car, and in two or three minutes were parked at the entrance to his house.

Once inside, Lane put the coffee on and began preparing bacon and scrambled eggs, while setting Lise to work preparing toast and slicing fruit. They talked animatedly all the while, touching a wide range of subjects, from the excellence of the organist at All Souls, to the most recent attempted genocide in sub-Saharan Africa, to the latest blockbuster special-effects movie. There almost seemed to be an unspoken agreement between them to stick with topics without direct personal reference, at least until they had overcome the initial awkwardness and unfamiliarity of being alone together in a very private setting.

It was not until they were well into the meal that Lane said, "So, now that you've had a couple of days to reflect on it, how are you feeling about your session with your father?"

Lise frowned thoughtfully. "It was an extraordinary experience," she said. "I never thought I could be so direct with him, could tell him how things really are with me, how I feel about his recent actions as a Trustee of the College.

"Of course, I didn't begin to get into the longer, deeper issues between us, though I did tell him they were there. This was just the first of what I hope will be a series of conversations, and sooner rather than later I want them to include my mother. But whether or not this is the beginning or the end is really up to them—depends on whether or not they are willing to risk the pain that goes with talking openly about such things. It's probably up to him, actually, given the fact that her habit has always been to follow his lead.

"But the discovery of my ability to be direct wasn't the only extraordinary thing about our meeting," Lise went on. "I could hardly believe the way he responded—the way he didn't respond may be a better way to put it."

"I don't understand" said Lane. "He did say something in response, didn't he?"

"Yes," said Lise, "but it wasn't what I expected. As you know, my father isn't accustomed to people saying no to him, least of all his daughter. And he certainly isn't accustomed to being told, in effect, that he has sinned against the light.

"Of course, he did offer some brief defense—told me that I didn't understanding the issues surrounding the anti-homosexual policy, that I wasn't competent to judge his views, his behavior. But when I didn't back down—in fact, when I came back even more forcefully, rejecting his condescension—he seemed to have nothing more to say. I expected him to be furious. At the very least, I thought he'd try to talk me down, but he didn't. Instead he was only silent.

"And he ended by telling me that he loves me. Somehow I don't think that was just a gimmick to make me feel guilty about my indictment—though he's entirely capable of that. I think he meant it."

"So what do you think is going on?" Lane asked.

"I don't know," said Lise. "He seemed—well, I guess 'vulnerable' is the word. I've never seen him quite like that before."

"Do you expect some kind of a more specific response from him?" Lane wanted to know.

"Yes," said Lise. "I asked him to reconsider the Trustee policy, and he said he didn't know what he would do. When we parted, he told me that he would be back in touch with President Kean on Monday morning. That's probably when they'll make an official decision about whether or not to go ahead. It's likely that I'll hear from him then, too.

"I guess I actually feel sorry for him," she added. "He must be in a very uncomfortable spot, even if it is of his own making."

Lane reached across the table and took both of her hands in his own. He said tenderly, "I can imagine how difficult all of this has been for you, and I admire your courage in saying what you felt had to be said. You are quite a remarkable woman, Lise Warner, and I like you very much."

"Oh, Lane," Lise said, "I don't know whether this is right or not, but I like you very much too. The fact that you are a professor and I'm a student confuses me, and I don't know how I ought to feel. I just know how I do feel. I find you more attractive than any man I've ever met. That may not sound like much of a comparison, since I haven't had close friendships with men. But I can't imagine that I could like being with anyone more than I like being with you."

Lane was almost overwhelmed by the fullness of her response. He leaned across the table and kissed her on the lips. Her mouth was warm and yielding. Lane said, "I know about that kind of confusion, because I've been experiencing it too. What is quite clear to me is that I care for you deeply. My suggestion is that we simply let our relationship go where it will go—not push it, not try to hinder it or second-guess it either. The fall term is almost over, and in a couple of weeks, at least the classroom complication will end for us. In the meantime, we should probably see each other out of the public view.

"Does that seem right to you?" he wanted to know.

"Entirely," Lise said. And this time she leaned across the table and kissed him in urgent confirmation.

That evening, after Lise returned to her dormitory room from supper in the College refectory, she had a call from the desk attendant. Apparently some one had come in, while everyone was at supper and no one was staffing the desk, and had left an envelope with Lise's name on it. Would she like to come down and get it? She would.

As she walked back to her room, she opened the envelope and found a single, hand-written page. She read:

For Lise

That head, that face,
That form, that grace,
That style, that glance,
That look askance,
That gentle touch,
That shy surmise
That gaiety
That lights your eyes,
That warming laugh,
That kindling smile,
That quiet strength,
That lack of guile,
That royal mien,
That common sense—
In these I scan
Love's lineaments.

It was signed, simply, "L."

*

Ellen and John Warner lived in a large, comfortable house in a
pleasant residential neighborhood in the capital city where John's
Baptist church was located. Rather than housing its minister and
family in a church-owned manse, the church provided him with a
substantial housing allowance so that he could develop equity in a
home of his own. They had lived here for seven years and had begun to think that this might be their home until John retired fifteen
years hence. Pastorates these days didn't usually last that long, but
it certainly wasn't unheard of, and things seemed to be going too
well for John Warner even to think of doing anything else.
Macauley College was only an hour and a half drive away, and his
recent election as the chairman of its Board of Trustees added dis-
tinction and satisfaction to the prominence to which he had already
risen, in the local community and in the national denomination, as

senior minister of First-Judson Baptist Church.

But on this Sunday evening, all that had been placed at risk. Two weeks earlier, Ellen Warner had told her husband that she was giving serious thought to leaving him. She hadn't made a final decision, she said, but she thought it only fair to warn him that the possibility was firmly in her mind.

John was stunned, speechless—a rarity for one whose profession was dedicated to utterance. Never, in the remotest corners of his mind, had it occurred to him that such a thing could happen. He had seemed to live a charmed life, and he had come to assume that he was invulnerable to the ills that other flesh is heir to.

His first thought was not about the prospect of losing his companion of 23 years. It was, rather, that if Ellen were to make good on her warning, everything he had worked to achieve would be down the proverbial drain. He would obviously have to resign his pastorate. Although she had said she had in mind a permanent separation rather than a divorce—she made it clear that there was no one else in her life for whom she wanted her freedom—he knew that, in the church circles in which he moved, it was an article of faith that a minister, especially a senior minister in a large church, would have a helpmeet to assist with the social obligations that were a requisite of the position.

When he was finally able to find his voice to ask Ellen what, in God's name, had led her to this craziness, he found that she knew the answer. "John," she said, "I don't know where you are. I can't find you in there any more. In fact, I don't know whether or not there is any 'you' to be found. But there's something worse, tragic as that is. I don't know where I am. I can't find me in here any more, and I don't know whether or not there is any 'me' to be found. I've spent my entire adult life wanting what you want, thinking what you think. Well, that's not good enough any more. While there's still time, I want to try to find out what I want, what I think. And I'm not sure I can do that with you.

"We haven't had a marriage for at least a dozen years. We've had simultaneity, but there's been no intimacy.

"Now," she concluded, "have I answered your question?"

He had been angry, pleading, patronizing, placating, but she didn't move a millimeter from her initial statement. Her response was only theme and variations. It finally became clear to John that, whatever decision she might ultimately make, she would make it without any help from him. Meanwhile, he could only wait and hope.

She said she would let him know as soon she could think it through.

Then at breakfast two days ago, as he was preparing to go to Macauley for his Friday morning confrontation with President Kean and lunch with Lise, she told him that she had made her decision and that she was ready to talk with him about it. He responded in exasperation, part continuing anger that she would dare to think of leaving, part frustration that she couldn't have brought it up at a worse time. The discussion would simply have to be put off, he said. He was expected at Macauley in an hour and a half. Furthermore, he told her, he couldn't deal with such a life-altering prospect when he had an emergency on his hands at the college, to say nothing the fact that he still needed to prepare for the preaching service on Sunday morning and the informal service on Sunday evening. So the discussion would simply have to be put off to another time, he concluded peremptorily.

He wondered whether she might have deliberately chosen the most difficult time of his week for this, just to irritate him, catch him off stride. The real reason he wanted the delay was a hope, however faint, that with these fresh reminders to her of his overriding importance, and with forty-eight hours intervening, the problem might yet go away.

He suggested that they wait until Sunday night to have their conversation, and she had agreed.

So when he had told Charles Kean that his late arrival for their Friday morning appointment had been caused by a "pastoral emergency," it was only partly dissimulation.

After John had returned from Macauley, he was either in his study Friday afternoon and evening and through the day on Saturday, working on sermon preparation, or on the telephone talking with members of the executive committee of the Macauley trustees. There had been a lengthy conference call that ran on toward midnight on Saturday. Sunday was taken up with routine church duties, so there would have been no time for them to talk before evening in any case.

Now nine o'clock on Sunday evening found Ellen and John together in the family room of their home.

"You've made a decision?" John asked.

"I'm going to leave you," Ellen said, matter-of-factly. "Not right away. That wouldn't be fair to you. You will undoubtedly need some time to figure out what adjustments you want to make in your own life, what you want to do personally, professionally. I've waited this long, I can wait another few months.

"And I don't intend to divorce you. You've always said you didn't believe in divorce, and I guess that's one place where I really do share your view. When the time comes, I'll ask for separate maintenance.

"My plan is to leave early in the summer, after Lise graduates. And of course, until the time comes for me to go, I don't intend to tell anyone—except Lise—of my decision. I'll go to see her in a day or two. Meanwhile, I'm sure you and I can make amicable arrangements to live acceptably in the same house."

"Where will you go?" John asked, his voice uncharacteristically flat.

"I'm not sure," said Ellen. "I haven't worked out all of the details. I may go to live with my sister Charlotte. She's been alone since Harold died, and I'm sure she would welcome the company. Besides, since she lives in Ames, I could go back to school—maybe study art history. I've always wanted to know more about the Impressionists. Their paintings seem so full of light and hope."

"Then there's nothing more to be said?" John asked, fearing the answer.

"There's nothing more to be said," Ellen replied.

MONDAY

CHAPTER SIXTEEN

BAD NEWS, GOOD NEWS

It was scarcely after seven o'clock on Monday morning when Charles Kean's telephone rang at home. John Warner was on the line. He would be at Kean's office by 9:30, and when he arrived he would convey to Kean the weekend decisions made by the executive committee of the trustees. Kean was to cancel any other appointments he might have made for the balance of the morning. After their conversation, Warner said he would take whatever time was necessary to prepare a statement for release by noon both to the faculty group represented by Dean Morton Emmons, and to the College at large.

The fact that Warner did not tell Charles Kean, in that brief call, exactly what the Trustees' decisions were, made Kean profoundly uneasy as he hung up the telephone. Moreover, Warner had issued peremptory instructions rather than making collegial requests, and that served to deepen the President's apprehension.

Charles Kean reflected that this wasn't starting out to be a very promising week.

The John Warner who walked into the President's office on the dot of 9:30 on this Monday wasn't the same man who had walked in on the previous Friday morning. Charles Kean noted the difference at once. The usual, somewhat fixed smile was gone, and the customary pastoral gloss seemed to have gone with it. Kean couldn't quite read Warner now. While there was decisiveness in his voice, the confident self-assurance that had been so irritating at times in the past was missing. Kean wasn't sure how to put those two things together, and the clash between them added to Kean's unease.

At least he hadn't long to wait for the Chairman to come to the point. Warner said, "I've been on the telephone to the Board's executive committee constantly over the weekend, both individually and in a conference call. Frankly, Charles, we think you've led us into a quagmire."

Kean began to protest. The policy on gays may have been his idea, he said, but after all, Warner had given it his full support, and members of the Board had voted to adopt it. But John Warner interrupted.

"I'm not trying to avoid the Board's share of responsibility for the mess we're in, nor indeed my own responsibility for it. We did, indeed, vote to enact the new policy. I now think that was a mistake, and if the issue were to come up today, I'd vote against it and urge other Board members to do the same."

"What's happened to change your mind?" Kean demanded to know.

"I'm not prepared to go into that in any detail. I haven't, in fact, changed my mind about homosexuality itself. I still believe that it is contrary to the law of God. But recent events in my own life have forced me to realize that having firm convictions of my own is one thing—is the core of selfhood. But insisting that others live by my convictions, by my detailed view of the world, is quite another—is, in fact, a formula for disaster. Rob Shaw's death was the result of just such an insistence, though for me personally not the most poignant result.

"In this insistence, your fault was no greater than my own. But you made your own distinctive contribution to the quagmire at two critical points: your egregiously inept reading of the faculty's readiness to accede to a policy of this kind, and your overweening desire to cultivate the good opinion of a student, by sharing with him a confidence that was too good to keep. Those were errors of judgment that a savvy administrator would not have made. You are not, I regret to conclude, a savvy administrator."

Charles Kean opened his mouth, wanting to make some kind of response, but no sound came out.

John Warner went on. "Here's what the executive committee of the Board has decided. First, the anti-homosexual policy will be expunged from the record. A trustee who had missed the original meeting pointed out, when I talked with him this weekend, that there wasn't a quorum present when we voted in any case, so the action was procedurally invalid under the best interpretation. After you and I have finished our conversation, I'll go into the Board room and prepare a statement from the Board to be transmitted to Dean Morton Emmons, telling him that the Board's original decision was invalid and that the issue will be permanently set aside. And I'll say that you fully support the recision."

Still there was no sound from Charles Kean.

"Second," John Warner continued, "since you have lost our confidence, we are asking for your resignation, to be effective nine months from today. That should give you time to arrange for a transition into some other line of work. We suggest that you think about returning to the corporate world, since we will not be in a position to give you a positive recommendation if you try to stay in higher education."

Now Charles Kean was clearly beyond words, and he sat as if he were stupefied.

John Warner wasn't finished. "I'll be resigning as Board chairman at about the same time," he said. "I expect to continue as chairman of the executive committee, to see that there is long-term follow-through on these decisions. But I'll be changing my own professional responsibilities, will be traveling a good bit, and will have only very limited time to give to the College. I've decided to leave the pastorate and to accept a full-time position as national chairman of my denomination's $50 million, five-year "The World Is Our Mission" campaign. It was offered once before and I turned it down. The offer was renewed a month ago and, until a couple of days ago, I was at the point of turning it down again. But now I've decided to accept.

"We don't want you to announce your departure now," Warner said in conclusion. "Wait six months, as I intend to do. There is no point in fueling speculation that Rob Shaw's death and our leaving are in any way connected."

The two men sat without speaking for a full five minutes. Then John Warner got up and walked out of the office.

*

Dean Morton Emmons had stationed himself at his office telephone from Monday mid-morning on, determined to be available should Charles Kean or John Warner call. But would they call? Had they really believed his threat of organized faculty resistance, of legal action against the Board and the College, if the Board persisted in its anti-homosexual policy? Would they have taken seriously his Monday-noon deadline?

Emmons wasn't at all sure that the telephone would ring. On the previous Friday morning, he had confronted Kean and Warner with a confidence he didn't really feel. Not that he was in any doubt that the proposed policy was thoroughly odious, reprehensible. That wasn't the problem. Rather, he didn't really know, when push came to shove, exactly how many faculty members could be counted on to stand firmly against the administration. And he had no idea whether or not the threatened legal action would even be accepted by the courts, let alone decided in favor of the plaintiffs. He merely knew that something had to be done to challenge the idiocy of the trustees, and that, whatever it was, he had to be a part of it.

And then, just after 11, his telephone rang. He let it ring a couple of times without picking it up, so as not to appear over-eager to the caller. When he answered, he found Anne Armstrong on the other end of the line.

"Any word yet?" she wanted to know. Emmons replied in the negative, and suggested that, delightful as it always was to talk to her, she should get the hell off the line in the event that Kean or Warner might be trying to reach him. Emmons promised to call Anne and the others as soon as he heard anything, and in any event by 12:15 if he had heard nothing. In that latter case, they could then meet as planned at 12:45 to decide on the next step. Anne hung up quickly, and Emmons continued his apprehensive vigil.

Twenty minutes later his telephone rang again, and this time he picked it up after the first ring, not caring how eager he might appear to the caller. He was surprised to hear the carefully modulated baritone of the chairman of the Board.

"Dean Emmons, this is John Warner. I have a response to the presentation you made to President Kean and me last Friday morning. I will spare you the details, but simply tell you that this past weekend, when the members of the executive committee of the Board reviewed the policy decision announced to the faculty by President Kean, we realized that it had been voted without the presence of a quorum. The action is therefore null and void. You have my personal assurance that it will not be formally reintroduced, and that student life administrators in the College will be instructed that they are not to proceed informally against any student on the grounds originally proposed in the policy. While I have claimed for myself the opportunity of informing you of this development, I can assure you that what I have just said is fully supported by President Kean. He will find his own ways to make that support clear.

"I will send you a copy of these remarks. In the meantime, you may communicate them to the faculty in whatever way seems most appropriate to you. I trust this fully addresses the concerns you expressed to us on Friday?"

"It does indeed," said Morton Emmons. "Thank you very much."

*

John Warner had one other task. He penned a note to Lise and, on his way out of town at noon, stopped to leave it for her at the dormitory desk. It read:

Dear Lise:

Point taken. Policy rescinded. Love,

Dad

*

The following memorandum was distributed to faculty mail boxes early on Monday afternoon:

Macauley College
Office of the Academic Dean
To: Faculty Colleagues
From: Morton Emmons

I am authorized by the Rev. Dr. John Warner, chairman of the Board of Trustees of the College, to tell you that the putative policy announced to us by President Kean at last week's faculty meeting has been found, by the Trustee executive committee, to be procedurally null and void and therefore without legal standing as a Board action. Furthermore, in reviewing the policy, the executive committee has concluded that the policy would have been ill-advised in any event, and that no further effort should be made, formally or informally, to enforce the action proposed in the policy.

Although I have been unable to reach President Kean directly, I have also been authorized by Dr. Warner to say that the President is in complete support of these more recent determinations by the Board.

I trust this will allay urgent concerns that have been expressed to me by members of the faculty since the announcement was first made ten days ago, and that we may now go about our academic business confident of the continuing integrity of Macauley College.

*October 27, 199_*

CHAPTER SEVENTEEN

INTERVENTIONS

When Morton Emmons's victory call reached him, Lane Thomas was at home having a pick-up lunch, an egg salad sandwich on week-old bread, and coffee left over from breakfast. It was remarkable how much better it all tasted after he finished the brief, mutually congratulatory conversation with Morton.

It suddenly occurred to him, as he ate, that mail had lain unopened on his entry table since Saturday. There had simply been too much going on for Lane to bother with a routine like opening the mail. There was seldom anything in it worth reading in any event, and the most personal- and important-looking missive usually turned out to be an expensively produced effort to sell him something he neither wanted nor needed.

But now, with the trustee business favorably concluded, he felt relaxed, unhurried, and mildly curious about what he might find in the pile. As he shuffled through the envelopes, one caught his eye. Its return address said "The School of Theology at Claremont, Claremont, CA 91711." That was where he had taken his doctorate. But I sent in my gift to the annual fund weeks ago, he thought. Schools are never satisfied. Always trying to wring another buck out of the alumni. And so thinking, he put the envelope aside without opening it.

After looking over a credit card bill, a renewal notice for *Christianity Today* magazine, another for *The Christian Century*, and a fund appeal from the Society for Values in Higher Education—Lane was a Fellow of the Society—and after skimming quickly through the latest issue of *The Washington Post National Weekly Edition*, he turned back to the Claremont envelope and opened it. He was surprised to discover a personal letter from the Dean. It said:

Dear Lane:

Recently the School of Theology has been given a substantial gift to endow a new doctoral program in Theology and the Arts. The anonymous gift comes from a long-time, dedicated supporter of the School. One of the provisions of the gift is that preference in selecting the first incumbent of the new chair should be given to one of our own doctoral graduates—as a means of affirming that our graduates are the equal of anybody's!

The successful candidate is to be appointed at the associate professor level, and with permanent financing assured by the endowment, the appointment will be offered with tenure.

Frankly, while we welcomed the new area of specialization, we were less enthusiastic about the restriction, until we suddenly realized that it would mean offering the position to you!

Your doctoral work, plus the articles you have published since leaving here on the subject of a theological aesthetic, seem to us to qualify you eminently to head up the new program.

Are you interested? Please let me hear from you at your earliest convenience. We want to settle the appointment within the next couple of months, so that the new program can get under way next fall. If you are interested, we'll arrange to fly you out for a two- or three-day visit.

Warmest personal greetings and good wishes to you.

It was signed, "Harry." Lane had studied with Harold McComber before McComber had become the Dean, and Lane knew him well. Lane was filled with a growing excitement as he re-read the letter. To have a position offered by one's alma mater was one of the ultimate compliments that could be paid to an alumnus.

Lane's mind raced ahead to the possible implications of this unexpected intervention in his personal and professional life. It would certainly solve the tenure problem here at Macauley. It would save him from life in a place whose social and religious outlook he could not share.

And there was something else—as events were progressing, perhaps the most important thing. After Lise graduated in the spring, it would be nobody's business what their relationship was, especially if they were both in Claremont, where she might well enter graduate study. She would have completed his class in a couple of weeks, and they would have greater freedom for the balance of the year to explore, to deepen, their relationship.

Lane could hardly wait to share this incredibly good news with Lise. He was sure she would welcome it, would see in it the same promise he was seeing. He reached for the telephone to call her, then suddenly remembered that she had a French language lab from noon until three.

He had scarcely removed his hand from the telephone when it rang. He picked it up at once, hoping that somehow it would be Lise. Instead it was Sandra Albright.

"Lane, any chance you and I could get together for an hour this afternoon?" Sandra wanted to know. "There's something important I'd like to talk with you about."

"In fact, my afternoon's free," said Lane eagerly. "And there's something important I want to tell you about, too," he added.

They agreed to meet in Sandra's office at All Souls Church at 1:30. Lane thought that would leave ample time, later in the afternoon, for him to meet Lise after her lab and tell her the good news.

"Euphoric" wouldn't have been quite adequate to describe Lane's mood as he approached the church. He could scarcely believe how things were coming together for him—well, for him and Lise, as he preferred to think of it. When Sandra Albright responded to his knock on her office door, he greeted her with a big grin and an enthusiastic hug.

"You'll never guess what I found in my mail today," he said to her at once. "I've been invited to consider a position back at

Claremont in a new Religion and the Arts graduate program. Associate professor, with tenure! I can hardly believe it. Talk about the solution to all of my problems. It must literally be a God-send!"

He decided not to tell Sandra the implications a move to Claremont might have for him and Lise. He had not explicitly discussed his feelings for Lise with Sandra, although her intuition may have discerned more than Lane intended to disclose on those occasions when she had seen him and Lise together. Women seemed to have a special sense about things like that.

"Congratulations! That's wonderful," Sandra said, and gave Lane a second hug to confirm her good wishes. "Do you think you'll accept? When would it begin?"

"I'll have to go to Claremont and endure the usual interviews and such. Of course, I'm not unknown there, and the letter from Dean McComber did sound like an outright offer. I need to know more before I make a decision, but it sounds terrific to me. If it still sounds that way at the end of my visit there, I'll will certainly accept. The position will begin next fall."

"Have you shared the information with Lise Warner yet?" Sandra wanted to know—and Lane thought she must have intuited something of what was active but unspoken in his mind.

"No. I only read the letter over lunch, and she has a French lab from noon to 3:00. I'll try to see her before the afternoon is up." He decided there was no point in masking his feelings altogether, so he said, "I really am eager to tell her. It may have implications for her as well as for me."

Sandra pointed Lane to a comfortable chair, and she sat nearby, away from her desk. "That's what I want to talk with you about," she said, and though she smiled warmly as she said it, there was a serious undertone in her voice.

"I'll have to risk the possibility that you may think me presumptuous. I am not only a friend of yours, and of Lise's. I also have a pastoral relationship to you and, as I have come to think, also to Lise. For reasons both of friendship and of pastoral concern, I feel a responsibility to raise some questions with you about Lise."

Lane was startled, uncertain of Sandra's meaning, but after a brief pause he managed to say, "I trust and respect you, both as a friend and as a priest, so of course I want to hear what you have to say. Has something happened? Is Lise in some kind of trouble that she may not know about?"

"Interesting you should put it that way," Sandra said. "I'm afraid that's exactly the problem. I'm worried that Lise is, indeed, on the verge of a kind of trouble she may not know about. I know you genuinely care about her, and precisely for that reason I hope you will agree to share my worry."

"Tell me," said Lane, though there was something in him that wasn't sure it wanted to know.

Sandra began. "Lise has shared with me that the relationship you and she have has become increasingly, and rather quickly, warm and close. I don't know the details, but I gather it hasn't yet become really intimate. That she is quite taken with you is no surprise. After all, you are a very attractive, very available man. Your intellect has impressed her, probably awed her a bit. And you've been very attentive to her, not only since the awful business with Rob Shaw but before that. She's flattered by your attention, drawn by your genuine attractiveness, and warmed by your warmth. And the difference in your ages isn't all that unusual. Many couples have managed a dozen years between them without feeling the gap.

Sandra paused briefly, and then asked, "Are you in love with her?"

For a moment Lane was unable to answer, unsure how he wanted to respond, his mind a melange. He was somewhat embarrassed to have his relationship with Lise examined in this way. But why should he be embarrassed? He hadn't done anything wrong. Of course he cared as much as Sandra about Lise's welfare. But what business was it of Sandra's to remind him of that? And where was she going with this line of conversation? Lane had an uneasy feeling that he wouldn't like the destination when they got there.

But he decided to answer Sandra's question directly, so he said, "Yes. I'm in love with her."

"That must be a wonderful feeling," was Sandra's surprising response. "She is lovely, bright, articulate, just the kind of woman who would attract you. It must be exciting to be aware of her responsiveness. You are certainly right to feel that way—if one person can tell another that his feelings are right! At the very least, your feelings are totally understandable."

Lane hadn't expected Sandra to understand. So perhaps his apprehensions about this conversation had been misplaced. And then Sandra said, "The fact that your feelings are totally understandable is really the problem. It would be easy for you to conclude that, because they are understandable, they can be trusted to guide your decisions, your actions. And that, I'm afraid, might be a serious mistake—a mistake especially for Lise, but also in the long run for you."

So, his apprehensions were not misplaced.

Sandra went on. "I know that what I am saying will be sharply disappointing to you, and that distresses me. But I have to take full responsibility for raising this issue with you, and I would like you to believe that I raise it because of my genuine affection and caring for you both. I realize you may not be able to believe that. And in any case, right at this moment you may not even be able to hear what I want to say to you. But I think I must make a good-faith effort anyway."

Lane sat back uncomfortably in his chair. Obviously he would have to listen to what Sandra had to say, whether he wanted to or not. A part of him wished he could escape whatever it was that was coming; but, in a peculiar way, a part of him did want to hear her out. It was as if he might be at the edge of some truth about himself that he dared not miss.

So he said, "Tell me what's on your mind."

Sandra said, "I want to tell you a story. It's about a young woman, an undergraduate in a college not unlike Macauley, who was majoring in psychology. She came from a family in which, though relationships were certainly not abusive, there was little warmth and few overt expressions of affection. Her inner world lacked definition, and she had been discouraged from exploring much of the outer world. Although in high school she had performed conventionally according to conventional standards, she had no inner standards, no aspirations of her own. She was one of those young people whom Edgar Friedenberg once described: an adolescent who, because she doesn't know what she's good at, doesn't know what she's good for."

Sandra went on. "Once in college and embarked on her major in her junior year, there began an amazing spiritual and intellectual transformation. It resulted primarily from the influence of her major professor, a talented psychologist, whose teaching awakened in her a passionate interest in ideas that she had never experienced before. She studied hungrily, and her brightness and enthusiasm and evident aptitude for psychological study won recognition from the professor. The importance of that mentor in her life grew with each new enthusiasm, and she began to experience a clarity and confidence about herself that she had never known before.

Sandra got up and walked to the window, all the while continuing the story. "Well into her senior year, she and the professor began to see more and more of each other outside of the classroom, and she was flattered by this added attention. She came to look forward to their wide-ranging conversations, in which she felt more like a peer than a student, her own views listened to with respect. They confirmed her own growing sense of value, of importance.

"And then one day in her senior spring, when they had gone to have one of those conversations during a long walk through a secluded park, the professor embraced her and kissed her. She was startled. Although she felt instinctively that the intimacy was inappropriate, she yielded, partly out of the warmth in her that his warmth had evoked, partly out of gratitude, partly out of fear that refusal might rupture the relationship that was giving substance to her life—might even jeopardize her academic record, her recommendations for graduate school."

Now there was no doubt in Lane's mind where all of this was going. It was not a place he wanted to be taken, but he continued to listen without interruption.

"When, in the summer following graduation, I broke off that relationship"—Lane was startled by the pronoun shift; it hadn't occurred to him that Sandra might be talking about herself—"I went into a deep depression. I alternated between longing and fury. What I longed for was the relationship the professor and I had before it became overtly physical. What I was furious about was the awareness that he had betrayed my trust, that he had used my vulnerability and woundedness and turned them to his own need, that he had used me to assuage his own woundedness. I was devastated, and for a time I lost the sense of self-worth that had grown in me up to the time of his betrayal.

"It took me more than a year in therapy to begin to recover it. That was ten years ago, and the recovery is still a part of my daily work."

"Was the professor really to blame?" Lane was hoping for some mitigation for his surrogate in Sandra's story. "Weren't you a consenting adult in that relationship?"

Sandra said, "Psychologists have come to the conclusion that, when dependency, trust, and a power differential are present, for the vulnerable party there can be no such thing as consent in any meaningful sense of the word.

"In fact," Sandra said, "in this unbalanced situation, even when the woman is the seducer, experience shows that eventually the result is disastrous for both."

Both were silent for a while. Then Lane said, "You think all that is what's happening between Lise and me?"

"My impression is that it hasn't quite gotten to a point of no return," said Sandra, "but I've had to wonder whether or not it may be heading in that direction. It's clear that Lise admires you, feels affection for you, is flattered by your attention, has been helped by you to find her own voice, is grateful to you, wants to please you. And all of that is good as far as it has gone—good for her as a student, affirming for you as a professor. It's what happens from here on that is problematic. I hope she can be spared the agony I've had to go through. I think you care about her enough to want that, too."

Again, both were silent.

Finally Lane said, "Thanks—I think."

TUESDAY

CHAPTER EIGHTEEN

TRANSITIONS

When Lise Warner returned to her dormitory room at the conclusion of her French lab on Monday afternoon, she found three envelopes in her mail slot at the desk.

One was the note from her father, reporting the decision that had been made concerning the anti-homosexual policy.

Another was a note from Lane Thomas, sent unobtrusively that morning through campus mail, saying that he had some exciting news to tell her, and asking her to give him a call before the end of the day.

A third was a letter from her mother, posted the previous Saturday and delivered by ordinary mail, and conveying the rather surprising news that her mother would be driving to Macauley the following day, Tuesday, to meet Lise, and asking Lise to leave on her mother's answering machine a suggestion of times during Tuesday that would be convenient for the two of them to meet.

The letter from her mother was surprising because, to the best of Lise's recollection, her mother had never come to visit her on the campus except when her father had business there.

She chose to respond to her mother's letter first, dialed the number, and left a message proposing that they meet at her dorm on the following morning at 10:30. She knew her roommate was a teaching assistant in a biology lab until one o'clock on Tuesdays, and that she and her mother could have the room to themselves for conversation. Then perhaps later they would go to lunch together.

She wasn't sure what to make of her father's note. While she was elated that the anti-homosexual policy was being rescinded, and that she might have had some influence on the recision— 'Point taken,' his note had said, the 'point' at issue presumably being her argument against the policy—she was troubled by the note's terseness. But there would be time enough to check that out.

Lane's note exhilarated her, even though she didn't know what to be excited about. It was enough that he was excited.

But by the time Lise received Lane's note, Lane had had his rather devastating conversation with Sandra Albright and was viewing the invitation to a Claremont candidacy with considerably less enthusiasm than when he had first written the note. While Claremont was clearly a singular professional opportunity, one that he could scarcely turn aside, he was no longer sure that it also represented the unique personal opportunity—the chance to put his relationship with Lise on a more promising basis—that he had initially thought it to be.

So that when Lise tried to reach him by telephone just before the supper hour on Monday, Lane was not as ready to talk with her as he had expected to be. He really needed more time to consider what Sandra had said to him that afternoon, to think through what the implications of Sandra's story might be for him and Lise—in fact, to make a fundamental decision about continuing or terminating their increasingly intimate relationship.

Lane was at home when Lise called. But precisely because he no longer knew what he wanted to say to her, he monitored calls on his answering machine in order to avoid talking to her until he could arrive at some greater clarity. He had never known such desperate ambivalence as he was now experiencing. In one moment, he thought that the only responsible thing—the only right thing to do for her sake—was to let her go, lest at some later time she should experience the personal devastation Sandra had described. And in the next moment, the prospect of letting go of the most exciting, fulfilling, healing relationship of his life was utterly intolerable, unimaginable, unacceptable.

Now on Tuesday morning, after a literally sleepless night, he was no closer to having resolved his excruciating dilemma than he had been on the day before. Although it would be hard to mask from her his depressed mood, he decided to go ahead and meet with Lise. She had no way of knowing, from his vague note, exactly what the exciting news was that he wanted to tell her, in any case. For all she knew, it could have been the recision of the anti-homosexual policy, since he could not have known about her father's note.

So at mid-morning on Tuesday, Lane left a message for Lise at her dormitory, proposing that they meet for coffee in the Campus Union at 3 o'clock. Much as he would have preferred to ask her to come to his house, the Union was neutral space and at least wouldn't make things any more complicated than they were already. He needed time to get Sandra's questions sorted out, one way or another.

It was fortunate that he had no Tuesday classes, Lane thought after he had telephoned the message. His nerves were shot!

*

When Lise arrived at her dormitory just before 10:30, she found her mother waiting in the reception lounge. Ellen Warner carried her 50 years lightly, and it was clear that Lise's litheness had been the gift of her mother's genes. Although Ellen's dress styles were always modest, self-consciously befitting the wife of a prominent conservative clergyman, there was a certain elegance in their simple lines, and her manner displayed a quiet dignity.

Mother and daughter greeted each other warmly, and Lise sensed in her mother a kind of energy that was unfamiliar.

As they walked, arm in arm, to Lise's room, Ellen said, "I'm so glad to see you. It's been two months, hasn't it? Too long for us to be apart. I've missed you."

"Thanks for coming," said Lise. "I was surprised to get your message, since you never drive down without Father. And I know you don't really like driving by yourself all that much. How nice for us just to have some time together."

Once in the room, which was comfortably furnished, they sat near each other, and Lise continued, "A lot has been happening here, as you probably know. In fact, much more than you know. You've probably heard about the suicide."

"Terrible," said her mother. "It's a parent's worst nightmare. I can think of nothing more tragic than losing a child." After a moment's pause: "Worse, really, than losing a spouse, I think."

"I'm afraid I was pretty hard on Father when he was here right after it happened," Lise said. "Somehow I doubt that he told you."

"He only said that you and he had talked and that you had some very strong feelings about the situation, but he didn't say what they were. I just assumed you were upset at the loss of a friend."

"It was certainly that," said Lise, "although Rob Shaw wasn't somebody I knew really well. But I was mainly upset—more than just upset; angry, really—at Father's role in the unfortunate business. Did he tell you that Rob was gay, and that the suicide was triggered by inside information Rob had that the Trustees were about to announce a policy to expel acknowledged gays from the student body?"

"He told me the suicide was related to the fact that the young man was gay, but he didn't say anything about a policy. He has never talked with me very much about Trustee matters," said Ellen. "Just thought I wouldn't be interested—or maybe wouldn't understand—I guess. I would have, though, I think—would have been interested, would have understood—given the chance. Was it true, that there was to be such a policy?"

"Yes," said Lise, "and Father was to have come here last Friday to make the official public announcement. I told him bluntly that I found such a policy thoroughly reprehensible, inhumane, unchristian, that I was ashamed of the part he had played in it, and that, for all practical purposes, he and the Trustees were personally responsible for Rob's death."

Ellen said nothing, but it was clear that she was startled by what Lise was telling her—too startled to make an immediate response. This was a Lise she had not known before, with a strength, an assertiveness, a clarity that was impressive.

Even more, Ellen thought, it was also a Lise whom John Warner must have found unfamiliar. How had it happened that these two women, his wife and his daughter, had suddenly come to life? she wondered. And at virtually the same time!

Ellen said, "I didn't know. That must have been hard—hard for you, hard too for him."

"It was hard," Lise agreed, "but I had the advantage. I knew what I wanted to say, and I had prepared myself to say it. Although, given the way he responded—or the way he didn't respond, didn't react angrily, was only nominally resistant to what I was saying—it was almost as if, in some way, he had been prepared, too."

"I think I can tell you about that," said Ellen. "In fact, it's the real reason for my visit. I was somewhat fearful of telling you this. But now that we have met again and have begun to talk, I think I needn't have been fearful at all."

Now it was Lise's turn to be startled. "What," she said anxiously. "Tell me."

"I've told your Father that I intend to separate from him early in the summer," Ellen said, more matter-of-factly than she felt.

Lise could hardly believe what she was hearing—not that her reaction to it was negative, but that she should be hearing it at all. Her mother separating from her father! Her mother, whom she had come to believe was incapable of having an independent thought, actually separating from her father. It so disturbed the established patterns of Lise's expectation that it was hard to take in.

After giving Lise a moment to absorb what she had said, Ellen continued, "I won't be seeking a divorce. I told him that, although over the years I have mimicked his views often without having any of my own, one place where he and I do agree is that divorce is wrong. So I will be asking for separate maintenance, perhaps going to live with your Aunt Charlotte in Ames. She's alone now, you know. Maybe I'll go back to university there in Ames, take up some study that I've always been curious about, like art history."

Lise was really getting a crash course in the new Ellen Warner. She had no idea that her mother might have been uncomfortable with echoing her husband's views, or was even capable of enough independence to know that that was what she was doing. And the fact that her mother had harbored an unfulfilled interest in art history was mind-boggling. She would have been even more astonished, had she known that Ellen, observing casually at first the books in Lise's own private library, had begun over time her own increasingly avid reading of Austen and Ibsen, of Hildegard and Julian, of Walker and Lessing and Mairs and Lamott, feeding on them as the manna of promise.

"What did you tell him?" Lise wanted to know. "I mean, what reason did you give him for wanting a separation?"

"I told him the real reason, which is that I haven't known who he really is for a very long time, and that I have lost track of myself, and that I'm not willing to live that way any longer. I do love him, I want you to understand—and I must be sure he understands that, too. But I cannot live with him; or to put it more directly and honestly, I don't want to live with him. At least not now. I don't rule that out for some future time, if I get myself sorted out and if I think he's done some sorting too. But I don't rule it in either. We'll just have to see what comes."

"And what did he say? How did he react?" Lise asked.

"Oh, he resisted at first; fulminated a little—but not as much as I expected he would; pleaded a bit; wanted me to feel sorry for him and relent. But when it became clear that I had thought it all through and had reached a firm conclusion, he realized that there was nothing for him to do but to accept my decision."

"And what will he do, do you think?" asked Lise. "Will the congregation accept a wifeless pastor? Even more, will they even let him stay in the face of the separation?"

"I'm sure he has no intention of waiting to find out. The denomination has offered him a national leadership position that would begin in the summer, and I think he intends to accept it. But it's important for him to tell you all about that himself. In any case, neither of us is saying anything publicly about this until spring.

"And something else important," Ellen added. "We have no intention of putting you in the middle of this thing. It's between John and me, and I'm sure that neither of us will attempt to recruit you to one side or the other. We know you love both of us, and we both love you. And your father and I will probably continue to love each other in important ways. I think what's happening will be for the good of all three of us. It will make us both more independent of each other and, oddly enough, more loving of each other."

Having at that moment the same spontaneous impulse, both women stood and hugged each other warmly. Lise's eyes welled with tears as she said, "You are really quite remarkable! I'm glad you are my mother!"

Lunch with her mother in the college Refectory over, and Ellen back on the road for the return trip home, Lise reflected that, whatever the rest of its hours might bring, this had already been an incredible day. The mother she had thought was a willing victim of her husband's ambition had taken charge of her own life and emerged as a real person after all. And the father she had thought was impervious to any appeals that did not arise from that ambition had turned out, under determined challenge by his wife and daughter, to be a vulnerable human being like any other.

Lise balanced unsteadily, but not unhappily, between laughter and tears.

*

Unwilling to brood inconclusively at home, and unable to concentrate on the work that awaited him at his office desk, Lane Thomas walked into the Campus Union an hour before the scheduled time for his appointment with Lise. He was relieved to find Jim Denison there, in the midst of a desultory cup of coffee.

Denison was reading, for perhaps the tenth time in twenty-four hours, the memorandum from Morton Emmons that had appeared in faculty mail boxes the previous afternoon. He had kept it with him because he could scarcely believe what it said. It confirmed for him what every good Roman Catholic should have known anyway, that the age of miracles is not past.

When Lane had gotten his own coffee and joined Jim at one of the tables, Denison said, "You know, when we got into this thing last week, in my heart of hearts I didn't think we could possibly win. I thought we ought to win, and I was sure we ought to try our damnedest to win, but I didn't really think it would work. I'm still not sure why it did. Somehow I can't see Charlie Kean giving in. He's neither principled enough nor smart enough. He'd be more likely to try to bull his way through, even if it meant ruining the china shop."

Jim chuckled and added that he thought Charlie Kean would probably like the metaphor.

He went on. "On the face of it, it seems too easy. It's almost as if there were some other influence, some other pressure on John Warner that you and I don't know anything about—and probably never will. Anyway, I must say it gives me somewhat more respect for him than I had before."

Lane agreed that the positive outcome was quicker and more complete than any of them had a right to hope. "Anne must be feeling particularly good about it," he said. "After all, she was the chief strategist, with Morton Emmons as a persuasive front man. The rest of us were just foot soldiers." And Lane chuckled at his own small metaphorical indulgence.

"If we're really going to flatter Charlie Kean by imitation," said Denison, "we should find some way to mix those metaphors— maybe something about 'a bull in the trenches.'" But he let it go at that, deciding that any kind of presidential 'flattery,' even if sardonic, was distasteful.

"Given the circumstances surrounding Rob Shaw's death," Jim Denison said, "we've had irrefutable evidence that this place is absolutely porous. Nobody, it seems, from the highest to the lowest, can keep a secret. Well, here's another. It was whispered to me this morning—in complete confidence, of course—that the faculty Committee on Promotion and Tenure has recommended that you be given tenure and is passing that recommendation on to the President and the Board. Has that bit of intelligence reached you yet?"

Lane said that it hadn't, and then he added, "While I'm grateful for the vote of confidence from my colleagues, I'm not celebrating yet. What you call the porosity of this place is likely to work against me. Sooner or later, Charlie Kean is bound to find out that I was one of the core of conspirators against him and the Board. And when that happens, good-bye tenure!"

What Lane didn't tell Jim Denison was that the tenure issue had become less important to him since receiving the letter from Claremont. While he would have liked to share his good news with Jim, it was clear that he wanted Lise to be the first to know, even though he was still undecided on how to present it to her.

And then suddenly, as if conjured up by his thought of her, Lise was there, standing beside him at the table. Unwilling to wait in her dormitory room, idly and impatiently, for the hour of their appointment to arrive, and activated by what her mother had told her, she had decided to pass the time in the Coffee Shop over a reflective cafe mocha. Entering by a side door, she had been unseen by the two men who were absorbed in their conversation. Surprised to find Lane already there, and deciding that the room was too small for her to be invisible for long, she thought it better simply to present herself.

"Excuse me, Professor Thomas," she said, discreetly formal. "I know I'm early for our appointment. I'll get some coffee and be nearby whenever your ready."

"Don't go," Jim Denison said quickly. "Time for me to leave anyway. Before the afternoon ends, I should probably spend an hour doing whatever it is philosophers are supposed to do—think about abstruse and irrelevant things, compose a prolegomenon to any future metaphysic, all stuff like that there." And with a friendly smile to both of them, he shambled off.

"I hope it wasn't wrong for me just to come up and present myself," said Lise, "but when I saw that you were here, I didn't know what else to do."

"No problem," Lane reassured her. "You did just the right thing in just the right way. Anyway, I consider Jim Denison to be a special friend. He's one of the good guys around here."

"As it turns out" said Lise, "I'm especially glad we're meeting now. I haven't had a chance to tell you that my mother came to see me this morning. Even though she has never driven down here by herself before, I thought what we would talk about would be pretty routine stuff—how things are going in my classes, how things are going in the parish at home—the sort of thing that makes me wonder, when it's over, why either of us bothered. But it wasn't like that at all. What she had to say absolutely astonished me. It made me sad, but at the same time I felt enormously encouraged by it.

"But wait a minute," she interrupted herself, "meeting was your idea, because you have something to tell, too. And here I am taking over."

"Not at all," Lane said, actually relieved not to have to plunge immediately into the Claremont business. "Tell about your mother. I want to know. Sounds like something really important."

"I guess the best way to say it quickly is that she's going to leave my father," Lise said. "I could hardly believe what she was telling me. It's not to be a divorce but a separation. And she's doing it because of emptiness—hers and his—an emptiness she's not prepared to settle for any more. She's come to the conclusion that she can't find out who she is until she distances herself from his influence, makes her own way, finds her own voice rather than simply echoing his.

"And it's not that she doesn't love him. She does. I'm convinced that this isn't merely a selfish, self-regarding move on her part. I think it's her loving way of forcing him to come to terms with himself, too; of forcing him to abandon his rote existence, to examine, to risk."

Lise was moved by this rehearsal of the morning's import, and Lane saw that there were tears in her eyes. He wished that he could hug her affirmingly, or at least hold her hand, neither of which was remotely possible in so public a place.

So he merely said, feelingly, "That's really quite remarkable!"

"Imagine my thinking that my mother lacked substance, lacked courage," Lise said, touching the corners of her eyes with the handkerchief Lane had handed her. "She's one gutsy person!"

"Jim Denison was wiser than he knew," Lane said. "When we were talking before you came, Jim had just said that the reversal of the Trustee policy decision almost seemed too easy, as if there were some other influence at work, especially on your father, beyond the faculty's threat of legal action. But, said Jim, if so, we'll probably never know what is was. Lise, you and I know what it was. It was the impact of two strong women in the Warner family, who have shaken John Warner out of his well-rehearsed responses and forced him to begin to look at life in a new way. You and your mother have altered his world permanently. He may not know where he's headed, but I suspect he's not where he was."

"Poor Father!" said Lise. "Change hurts, even when it's in the right direction."

For a moment both of them sat quietly, reflecting on the strange turn events had taken. And then Lise said, "But you have some news. I want to hear it. What's happened?"

Ready or not—and he wasn't—this is it, Lane thought.

"It hardly matches the importance of what you've been telling me," he said. "I've had a letter from the Dean at Claremont in California. I think you know that's where I took my doctorate. He has offered me an opportunity, beginning next fall, to help create a new graduate program in Religion and the Arts, with an advancement in rank from where I am here, and tenure on appointment."

"Oh, Lane!" Lise's enthusiasm made her forget that they were in a very public place and that her informality might be overheard. "How wonderful for you! You're going to accept, aren't you?"

"That's certainly my strong inclination," Lane said. "I probably don't have much of a future here, given my differences from the administration. And once word gets around that I had something to do with resisting its anti-homosexual policy, my position is likely to be even more tenuous.

"In any case," he added, "I'm asked to come to Claremont for some conversations about the new program and my possible role in it, so I won't make a decision until I've done that. I'm planning to fly to California at the end of the week, be there for full days on Friday and Saturday, and then fly back here on Sunday. In fact, I've got to see my chairman, Professor Dwight, yet this afternoon to let him know that I'll miss our class on Friday. I'm planning to ask Sandra Albright to substitute for me. Dwight will probably hate the idea of having a lesbian giving even a single lecture on the campus. But she's so obviously qualified, with her doctorate from Chicago. And besides, with the administration's policy reversal only days old, I doubt that he and the President will want to make Sandra an issue."

"I'm glad I'll be graduating in June," Lise said. "With you gone in the fall, I wouldn't want to be here anyway."

Was that statement really an implied question? Was Lise really asking him to tell her how he thought his move to Claremont would affect their relationship beyond the end of the college year? But he couldn't do that, at least not now. He needed more time to reflect on the hard things Sandra Albright had said to him. So he had to pretend not to hear any such implication, to take her comment at face value simply as a student's compliment to her teacher.

"Thanks. That's nice to hear," he said. And then wanting to leave before any more implications were raised, he added, "I've got to be on my way to Ralph Dwight's office, if I'm going to catch him before he leaves for the day. He'll probably think I'm not giving him enough notice as it is. But I'm not going to ask him if I can make the trip to California. I'm going to tell him I'm going. He'll probably be relieved at the prospect of getting rid of me permanently in any case."

As they said their good-byes, Lane promised to give Lise a full account of his trip the following Monday, since he wouldn't arrive back from California until late on Sunday night. "Of course, as usual we'll see each other in class tomorrow morning," he reminded. Lise wished him luck and good traveling, and they parted with a handshake that lingered slightly, though not enough for anyone nearby to notice.

WEDNESDAY

CHAPTER NINETEEN

REACHING CONCLUSIONS

On Wednesday morning, Lise rose early, went to her desk, and wrote the following letter:

Lucinda Stone Hall
Macauley College
*October 29, 199_*

Dear Father:

I would prefer to be saying these things to you in person, and I hope there will be a chance for us to talk, face to face, before too many days.

The first thing is to thank you for the note you dropped off here before leaving the campus on Monday. And not just for the note itself, but also for telling me the decision you had reached on the Trustee policy we discussed at lunch on Friday.

I am, of course, grateful for the outcome. Even more, I'm grateful that you really did hear me, not just indulgently as your daughter, but as a person—perhaps as a peer—whose views were worth taking seriously. I feel as if I have a new relationship with you now, and I like the way that difference feels. I want to thank you for helping it to happen.

You probably know by now that Mother came to see me yesterday, and told me about her own recent decision. That's the other reason for this letter—not merely to let you know that I know, but to tell you that I'm sorry for the pain that decision may—undoubtedly will—cause you.

I love you both. I admire Mother's courage in striking out on her own—it can hardly have been easy for her. And I admire your willingness, in response, to strike out into the unknown, too, by taking on a new kind of job—that can't have been easy, either.

I guess what I want to say is that both of you have given me really strong examples of how mature women and men can reshape their lives. It's a maturity I don't yet have, but because of your examples, I'm more likely to achieve it.

Let's meet soon. I love you.

Lise

She was careful to see that the occasional tear didn't stain the writing paper. She posted the letter on her way to breakfast.

First thing on reaching his office at 8:45 on Wednesday morning, Ralph Dwight dialed the direct line into President Charles Kean's office. In a deep funk, Kean had kept himself virtually incommunicado there since his unhappy meeting with John Warner on Monday, instructing his secretary to make no appointments and to put through no calls. She was to record messages and requests, and he would see what he wanted to do with them in due—or perhaps in undue—time.

Unwilling to tolerate the insistent ringing of his desk telephone, which had been activated by Ralph Dwight's direct call, Kean was at least relieved to hear Dwight's familiar intonations on the other end. It could be worse, he reflected—it might have been Morton Emmons, or, God forbid, John Warner with more bad news.

"Late yesterday I had a visit from Lane Thomas," Dwight began eagerly and without preliminary. "It looks as if we're to be rid of him, even without the plan you and I discussed last week."

Charles Kean was uncharacteristically silent on the other end of the line. Usually he took over a conversation, but now he made no response. So Ralph Dwight continued: "Lane came to see me late yesterday to say that he'll miss his Friday class this week. He's been invited to Claremont for an interview, and if all goes as he expects it to, he'll be accepting an invitation to join their graduate faculty in the fall, with an increase in rank and with immediate tenure."

Still there was no response from Kean. "Charles, are you there?" asked Dwight.

"Of course I'm here," said the President testily. "I have the impression you're going somewhere with all of this. When you get there, I may have something to say."

"Yes, well," said Dwight, somewhat disconcerted by Kean's odd mood, "I just thought—that is, as you know, you have on your desk a favorable recommendation from the faculty committee on Thomas's tenure and promotion to Associate Professor. And it occurred to me that, if he's going to leave anyway, we can save ourselves the grief of turning down the recommendation, which would probably just create another anti-administration fuss in the faculty. Why not let him have it? Once he's gone, you can do whatever you want to do with that position in Religion."

Charles Kean wasn't about to tell Dwight that he—Kean— wouldn't be around next year to do anything at all with the position, John Warner having asked for his resignation by spring. At the same time, Kean certainly wasn't averse to avoiding another bruise, especially if the compromise it took to avoid it were virtually painless.

So Kean said, "Yeah, okay. I'll ask the Board to give him a pass, explain that Thomas is doing us a favor by leaving. Point out that actually it will be a net plus for us, one of our teachers being invited to accept a position at a prestigious university. And anyway, we'd look pretty stupid to refuse tenure, and then have a place like Claremont come along and just hand it to him."

So they agreed to wait until Lane Thomas returned from his California trip; and if, as expected, he should then announce his intention to resign from Macauley at the end of the academic year, Kean would recommend that the Board approve Lane's advancement.

Thank God something is going right for me, Kean thought as he put the telephone back in its cradle. It isn't much, but it's something!

*

Lane Thomas had called Sandra Albright at home on Tuesday night to invite her to take his Friday morning class on "Theological Issues in Contemporary Literature" while he was in California. She seemed pleased to accept the invitation, and they had agreed to meet for lunch the following day to discuss the details. Sandra proposed a brown-bag in her office as a quiet and unhurried venue for that discussion. So on Wednesday morning, before he left for the campus, Lane had made a tuna sandwich and put a few chips in the bag with the sandwich. Now they were seated comfortably in her study at All Souls Church, sharing the coffee Sandra had brewed in anticipation of his arrival.

"Since this is a rather last-minute invitation, I want you to do whatever you're comfortable with in Friday's class. I can tell you what I had scheduled myself to do, but under the circumstances, that needn't constrain you," he told her.

"What's on the syllabus for Friday?" she wanted to know.

"Well," said Lane, "I've had the class reading Dietrich Bonhoeffer, especially his *Letters and Papers from Prison*. As you know, one of his themes is, that to be a Christian is to 'participate with God in the suffering of the world.' Since the point of the course is to examine how similar themes may be treated in so-called secular literature, and to create an imaginary dialogue between the two, I had intended to examine Bonhoeffer's theme in the light of Graham Greene's *The Power and the Glory*. It seems to me that the 'whiskey priest' in Greene's novel has a similar view of his own vocation. Or if you prefer, you could do the theme of sin and salvation in the novels of Walker Percy."

"The Bonhoeffer-Greene connection is a very interesting

match," said Sandra. "It happens that I've been reading Bonhoeffer again recently, and I'm pretty familiar with Greene, so a review of the novel will only take an hour or so. Why don't I plan to follow the syllabus. That way you and the class won't lose any time."

"That's very generous," Lane replied. "They'll love the change of voice, the different perspective you're bound to bring. In fact, my only fear is that they won't welcome my return!"

"At least one person will," said Sandra.

While the conversational transition was hardly unexpected, Lane had dreaded it. He had scarcely thought about anything else since Sandra told him her cautionary tale on Monday. Had it only been two days? It seemed like an eternity. Lane knew what he had to do—had to do, at least, if he really loved Lise as much as he told himself he did. But whether or not he could bring himself to do it was something else again. It would be the hardest thing he had ever done in his entire life. And it would cause pain to Lise too, he was sure. She had made no outright profession—nor had he, except to Sandra—but he was in no doubt that her feelings were very much like his own. And somehow he couldn't imagine himself telling her that a renunciation of their relationship, if it came to that, was for her own good, that it hurt him as much as it hurt her. Those were the kinds of things one said to ease his own conscience, not to make things easier for the other person.

"I'm afraid you're right," Lane said in direct response to Sandra's comment. And then, because he didn't know what else to say, he simply told her what had just then been running through his mind.

Sandra was her usual empathic self. "I can imagine the struggle—the virtual warfare—that must be going on inside," she said. "And it's certainly not my intention to make things any more difficult for you than they are. I'll continue to be your friend whatever you decide to do. I simply wanted you to know, out of my own painful experience, what the risks may be of continuing in the way you and Lise seemed to be going. And having said that, I don't intend to raise the question again. Of course, I'm here for you, should you decide that you want a foil for your feelings, but I'll leave that entirely to you."

Lane thanked her for caring and for understanding, and thanked her too for willingness at short notice to stand in for him with his class on Friday morning. When he stood to shake hands with her, indicating an end to their conversation, she gave him a hug instead, which he accepted and reciprocated gratefully.

*

As it turned out, Lane Thomas wasn't Sandra Albright's only visitor on this Wednesday afternoon. Lise Warner had left her dormitory shortly after lunch, headed for the park path that ran along the river not far from the campus, and had spent nearly three hours walking, trying to sort through the implications of the remarkable things that had happened since the weekend—to the college, to her mother and father, to Lane, and of course, by extension to her as well.

Her preoccupation was so intense that she was scarcely aware she had left the park until she suddenly found herself approaching the corner on which All Souls stood. Once she realized where she was, it occurred to her that her arrival at this place might not be so adventitious after all. If she had not intended this final destination in her conscious mind, perhaps it was no accident that her feet had brought her here where she might find, in Sandra Albright, a cohering wisdom for gathering the strands of recent happening into some manageable shape.

Without hesitation she entered the church and, finding Sandra's study door, knocked somewhat tentatively. Sandra opened without delay and greeted Lise with a warm smile, grasping her two hands and drawing her into the familiar room.

"What a nice surprise!" said Sandra, and pointed Lise to a comfortable seat. "What brings you here?"

"Actually I'm not sure," said Lise. "I've been out walking since just after lunch. I'm not wearing a watch and I have no idea what time it is. I now realize that I have been walking with no sense of time or place. I certainly had no intention of coming here to see you without an appointment. But then all of a sudden I found myself approaching the church, and I just walked in, as if I had intended to come here all along. Perhaps I did, without knowing it."

"Well, if it matters," said Sandra, "it's half past three, so you've obviously had quite a walk. And you needn't concern yourself about coming without an appointment. Fortunately I'm not occupied with anyone else, and you know that I'm always glad to see you.

"So. Tell me what's going on."

Lise did. She talked about the note from her father, and her delight that there had been a remarkably—indeed, surprisingly—favorable resolution of the Trustee policy-issue. She spoke of the hardly believable news her mother had brought her, of her admiration of strengths she had never known her mother possessed, and of her sadness at the pain her father must be experiencing. And she talked of the prospect that Lane would likely be moving to Claremont at year's end.

Sandra expressed surprise, especially at the family developments. "All of that's an enormous lot for anybody to have to cope with all at once. How are you managing?" she asked.

"For the most part, pretty well," said Lise. "Although the retreat by my father and the Trustees came more quickly and easily that I could have dreamed, it was what I wanted, and I've felt enormous relief that there won't be another tragedy like Rob Shaw's. I wish Rob could know that his death dramatized the senselessness, the wrongness, of the proposed Trustee policy, and mobilized the opposition to defeat it in a way that mere argument could never have done.

"As for what's happening to my parents," Lise went on, "that's more complicated, of course. My mother has made a courageous decision, and in spite of its promise it must be painful for her. I know it is for my father, in spite of his having found a way to redirect his career with minimal loss to his public standing. It's harder for him because he didn't choose the pain as she did, and I think it is likely to become even more painful for him as time goes on and he feels the emptiness left by my mother. I suspect that, for both of them, pain is the price of growth, whether chosen or not."

Lise hesitated now, and Sandra decided not to fill the silence. She realized that there was one remaining item among the new developments Lise had listed when she began her recital, and Sandra had no intention of naming it.

After a space, Lise said, "But the situation with Lane is different. I knew what I wanted to happen at the College. And even though I could never have anticipated the form they took, I also knew what changes I had hoped for in my parents' lives, and in my relationships with each of them. But I haven't really known how I wanted my relationship with Lane to work out. I just let it happen without thinking much about it, because it was so new and so fulfilling. He gave me confidence in myself, and he gave me a warmth and tenderness that I had never felt before with a man. So I didn't think—or feel—too far beyond the very real pleasures of the moment."

Again Lise hesitated. Then she said, "I have an intuition that he will ask me to go to Claremont with him. After all, I'll be graduating in June, and we would be free then to pursue our relationship more intimately without teacher-student constraints. And I must admit that that possibility is strongly attractive to me—that Lane is strongly attractive to me. He is the most caring man I have ever met. More than that, he has treated me like an intellectual peer— has taken my ideas with real seriousness. He has all but said that he's in love with me. And I think I love him, too—if I know what love is. I doubt that I'll ever find anyone who is easier to be with, who is more affirming to be with. So if he asks me to go with him, it will be very easy for me to say yes.

"And yet...." Once more a hesitation.

"Am I ready to move from recent undergraduate to faculty wife, with virtually no transition between the two? Leave my own world, enter fully into his? He's ten years older than I am. Joining his world would be like instant adulthood, giving up most of my young-adult years. I'm not sure I really know myself very well yet—know much about the way the world works. Most other women my age have had a few years to try on different identities, to find out which kinds of relationships work for them and which don't, to test which kinds of commitments they can live with and which they can't. Until now, my life has been much more restricted. Even with a late start, it may still be important for me to take time to experiment and risk, before settling in to one relationship, before settling for one future."

"On the other hand...." Again, silence.

Suddenly Lise stood up. With a confidence and energy she had not shown when she first arrived, she now said to Sandra, "This time with you has been terribly important, because I now know what I'm going to do. Without your help, I could never have come to a decision. I can't begin to tell you how grateful I am." And before Sandra could reply, Lise had drawn her up out of her chair, gathered her in a warm and vigorous embrace, and strode purposefully out of the room.

Once the door was closed, an astonished Sandra sat down again. What decision had Lise come to out of these moments together? The way Lise had described the alternatives didn't seem to suggest a clear choice. "And whatever decision she has made, it's no thanks to me," Sandra thought. "I scarcely said fifty words to her during the entire time we were together, none of them substantive."

"If I ever get smug about my talent for dispensing life-altering advice," Sandra thought, "I'll remember this afternoon!"

MONDAY

CHAPTER TWENTY

RESOLUTION

It was ten minutes to eight when he left the house. He knew he would be late, and he wasn't sure the students would still be in the classroom when he arrived.

Again!

The departure of Lane's flight from California the previous night had been delayed because of dense fog, and after missing his connecting flight at O'Hare, he hadn't arrived back in town until after 1:00 a.m. By the time he crawled into bed, it was nearly two o'clock. In addition to the lateness, the emotional impact of those weekend days at Claremont, though entirely favorable, had taken their toll, and he was exhausted. So he had slept through the alarm and woke to find that it was already 7:40 and that there was no chance of his arriving at the class by the scheduled hour. He skipped the usual morning shave, hustled into his clothes, and headed out as quickly as he could pull himself together.

Arriving at Founders Hall, now past the mythological ten-minute limit, he took the steps two at a time on his way to the second-floor classroom. It would probably be empty, he thought. Except perhaps for one.

He opened the door and stepped apprehensively in. She was there.

Again!

Five days and nearly three thousand miles had separated them. For Lane it had been a time of emotional extremes. Elated by his reception at Claremont, and excited by the new professional prospect it offered, there had also been times of depression, especially on the four-hour flights to California and back, as he tried to sort out feelings and fears.

By the time he had landed at Ontario International Airport

near Claremont on Thursday evening, it was clear to Lane that, however painful it might be for him—and it was excruciating even to contemplate—he simply had to find some acceptable way to return his relationship with Lise to the simple student-teacher status it had when the fall semester began. He did love her, he was sure of that. And this was one of those tragic situations in which love required renunciation. He had to let her go, to free her from the deeper entanglement into which she might be beguiled by admiration and gratitude, and which at some later time she might come to despise, if Sandra Albright was right.

At thirty-thousand feet over Southern California, Lane wept silently at the prospect of lost loveliness.

On the return flight, Lane's preoccupation had been, not with his own feelings but with Lise's. He tried, without success, to imagine how he could say to her, "I love you and I'm letting you go." What kind of sense would that make to one as young and inexperienced as she? It was only with the greatest difficulty that it even made any sense to him. She would be disappointed, would feel perhaps that he had misled her, might be devastated by his withdrawal. But recent events, especially in relation to her mother and father, had shown Lise to be increasingly strong and resilient, and he was confident that eventually she would recover. In the meantime, it would be rough for both of them.

And now here she was, the only student who had waited for him forgivingly, in spite of the lateness of his arrival.

His feelings were in a muddle, partly apprehensive at what lay ahead of them, partly warmed by her presence. All he could think to say, inanely, was "Imagine meeting you here!"

Again!

"Welcome back," she said, with a luminous smile that melted some of his resolve. In spite of the classroom setting, they hugged, briefly and self-consciously, and then sat down to talk.

"Did it go well? Do you like the job. Are you going to take it?" she asked.

"Yes, yes, and yes," said Lane with a gentle laugh. He was entranced by her eagerness. "I was given the royal treatment. The job sounds great. It takes time to get enrollments and momentum in a new program, so I'll teach "Introduction to Theological Aesthetics" in the fall, probably pick up another course or two in philosophical theology during the year, and in the meantime begin to develop other specialized courses that eventually will become a doctoral sequence. And I signed a letter of acceptance on Saturday night."

"How wonderful for you," Lise enthused. "Actually, how really wonderful for them! They don't know how lucky they are to be getting you."

Lane said, "I feel as if I've been saved from sheol, the afterworld the Psalmist always prayed to be delivered from because it was dim and grim. I like my students and some of my colleagues here, but I had begun to think this place was a dead end for me professionally. Suddenly I've discovered that there is life after Macauley College!"

And then he added, "Enough about me. What's been happening to you in the last five days?"

"In fact, there is something I want to tell you about," Lise said. "It's not something I'm prepared to share very widely—not with my roommate, at least not yet. I may tell Sandra Albright, since it's connected with some things she and I have already talked about. But I've learned that I can trust you more than anyone I've ever known."

"Sounds pretty important," said Lane, with mixed curiosity and apprehension.

"Well, it's nothing really major," she said, "but it is a step for me, and I think it's a step in the right direction."

"You certainly have my attention," he encouraged.

"While you were away," Lise began, "I got to thinking about recent events on the campus, and especially about Rob Shaw. I thought about his roommate, Steve Braithwaite, who first found Rob and reported his death. And I thought how terrible it must have been for him.

"Well, Steve is in my Shakespeare seminar. I haven't known

him very well. We just sort of smile and nod whenever we see each other. And it occurred to me, on the way out of class on Thursday, to speak to him, tell him that I'd been thinking about him, how much I regretted all that had happened, how hard these recent days must have been for him.

"So he suggested we go over to the Campus Union for coffee. And as it turned out, we talked for an hour and a half. It was quite remarkable. I mean, I don't know where the time went, but we just seemed to have a lot to say to each other.

"And then he said, 'How about having supper with me in town on Saturday night?' It seemed quite natural for me to say yes, so I went. And I had a really great time.

"You know," Lise went on, "I haven't dated at all since coming to college. I'm pretty inexperienced, and I think I had been a bit frightened of being with men. But being with Steve wasn't frightening at all. It seemed just right. So we're going to see each other again, probably take in a movie on Wednesday night.

"Mainly what I want to tell you," said Lise, looking intently at Lane, "is that I have you to thank for my new willingness to risk being with a man. You have given me a confidence in myself that I have never had before. I discovered that I could trust you, that I was not afraid to be with you. More than that, that I liked being with you. And those were new feelings for me. I'll never be able to thank you enough for helping me open my life to new possibilities."

She reached over and kissed Lane on the cheek.

He was speechless. Disappointment and relief competed within him; grief and joy were in collision. What he had dreaded to do, she had done for him. He was deeply saddened that he had lost her as a lover, but he was deeply grateful that she had been, would be, unharmed by him. He would miss the subtle intimacies they had begun to share, but perhaps he had helped her open herself to new relational possibilities—with her father, her mother, and now with Steve Braithwaite. In fact, perhaps he too had been opened to new relational possibilities.

Then he said, "Anything I may have given you was simply a return on what you have given me—the gifts of your trust, your confidence, your friendship. You are a remarkable woman, Lise Warner. I will always think of you as one of the really important people in my life." And he reached over and returned her kiss.

They both seemed to know that it was time to go. There was nothing more to be said, at least in that place, in that moment. So they walked silently out of the classroom, down the steps to the entrance, and out of Founders Hall.

"See you Wednesday in class," Lise said, taking his hand warmly.

"Right," said Lane, "see you then."

After his draining encounter with Lise, Lane felt the need for a strong restorative cup of coffee, and he headed for the Campus Union to get it.

There, sitting at a table by herself, was Anne Armstrong. Lane pulled up a chair and sat down. "Anne," he said, "things have been so hectic around here lately that there's hardly been any time for fun. What do you say we have supper together on Saturday night, then take in the concert by the Minnesota Orchestra at the Civic Auditorium?"

Anne grinned. "I thought you'd never ask!" she said.